# Just The Honeymoon

JEREMY DORFMAN

Printed in the United States of America

ISBN 978-0-6922767-2-3

Book design by Jenelle Rittenhouse

Cover design by Momir Borocki

This work is inspired by true events. Names, dates, locations, and details of the story have been changed for the purposes of the narrative.

**ACKNOWLEDGEMENTS**

*Thanks to all who made this book possible - John Liang, Carl Amari, Jessica Bennett, Honor Beyer, Jenelle Rittenhouse, and Jill Dorfman, as well as a special thanks to those who lived the real lives that inspired our story.*

*Inspired by a*
*True Story*

# PROLOGUE

## i: August 24, 2013

Kara slipped off her treacherous high heeled shoe and dipped her toes in the soft, cushiony sand. Her foot sunk into the pearly white grains. Her skin was massaged by the perfect beach. She thought about the world of difference between the soothing Hawaiian sand and the hard, uninviting dirt of the Mexican desert where people she had known had fought thirst and heat exhaustion to make their way into the States. Against her face was a cool ocean breeze instead of a dry, all-consuming stillness. On her body was a silk satin white dress instead of a cotton, sweat soaked tee shirt.

Kara took a long look around the heavenly paradise where she found herself.

The almost inconceivable beauty struck her differently than it had when she arrived, filtered through this moment of fragility. It struck her as falsely reassuring. Human life was no different here than it was in any other place. Not really. Splendor only distracted from life's uncertainties. It did not remove them.

Kara shut her eyes, dipped her head, and began to pray.

*Dear God,* she said silently. *This is Kara Gomez. I need your help.*

*I do not know if what I'm about to do is the right thing. There are so many factors. There is my father. There is my family. This is as much for me as for them. A child is supposed to help her parents. Is this not correct?*

*But it is also for me. I know this. I want to keep living in the U.S. And ... I*

1

*want him. I have hopes. I have dreams. Should I not pursue them in any way I can?*

She paused for moment, perhaps waiting to see if God would respond, then continued.

*I am trying to do what is right. I want to do something good. You know this. You must.*

*I am confused. I am nervous. Please God, give me your strength and guidance. Show me the way forward.*

Kara breathed in the crisp Hawaiian air. She stood silently for a long time. Her thoughts slowed down. She thought of running off. She would travel the beaches for the rest of the day, then at night she would vanish into the Hawaiian sunset, consumed by the oranges and yellows and pinks. She would say goodbye to her human cares forever.

But this was impossible. And what was more – it was not what she wanted. What she wanted was to marry the man who waited for her just across the beach.

She bowed her head, feeling she had done all she could to appease the higher power, and said, "Amen."

They would be wondering where she had gotten to. No more waiting. It was time.

Kara slipped her shoe back on and walked past the palm trees which separated her from the tiny wedding ceremony. At her appearance the photographer hit the play button on the iPod speaker system and the sounds of "Here Comes the Bride" filled the air.

The priest smiled at her as she made her way across the beach, but she was too busy looking at her future husband to notice.

Dan's eyes were undoubtedly consumed by love. It reassured her to see the way he looked at her as she approached. No matter what had occurred before, right here, right now, he wanted to marry her. She was sure of it.

Looking at the man she loved, all her worries fell swiftly away. She felt happy.

*Maybe it will all work out*, she thought, hopefully. *Sometimes in life things work out.*

*Don't they?*

## ii: January 10, 2013

Dan looked at the accusing calendar book with its unmarked January 10th page and wondered how his sister was celebrating her birthday. He didn't need a written reminder to know the significance of this particular date.

He imagined that she and Kevin and the kids probably would probably go out to some Vietnamese restaurant, or maybe Thai. She loved all the branches of the Asian food family tree. He pictured little Annie and Matt sharing some fried noodle dish with their mother, giving her dollar store presents they bought with their small allowances.

Dan considered calling Sue for the first time in over two years. Never one to mull over decisions long, he immediately decided against it. Her birthday was probably the worst day to end their silence. There was no way the phone call would be tension free. It was highly likely they wouldn't reach any common ground and they would hang up angrier at each other than they had been before he had dialed.

The last thing he wanted to do was ruin his sister's birthday. He wanted her to be happy. He wanted her to enjoy herself with her family. Maybe he would call her sometime soon on a less emotionally charged occasion.

They had ostensibly stopped talking because of his break up with Rebecca. Dan had been with Rebecca for eight years and Sue couldn't begin to comprehend why Dan would end it. She had begged him for at least five of those eight years to marry Rebecca and bring her into their family. She *adored* Rebecca. They bonded in a way that Dan and Sue never had.

When Dan told Sue that he and Rebecca had broken up she screamed at him for what must have been twenty minutes. She refused to even listen to any of his explanations. She cut him off each time he tried to assert his position.

Rebecca had decided she was no longer okay with the idea of never having kids. She wanted a family, Dan explained.

"So start a family!" Sue yelled.

"I've told you, Sue. I don't want kids," he said.

"Do you still love her?" Sue asked.

"Yeah," said Dan quietly. "I do."

"Well sometimes when you love someone you have to do things you don't want."

"It's not that simple."

"Try to explain it to me."

"I still love her but I know that I won't always. We just have different priorities."

"You're being immature Dan!"

Eventually Dan, who almost never lost his composure, started yelling as well. He said some things he regretted.

"What do you want Sue?" he said. "For me to rot in a boring marriage like you and Kevin have? To live a pathetic miserable life like you do? I'm sorry but your life just doesn't appeal to me. I'd rather live my own."

He felt bad about saying it almost immediately. He felt even worse when Sue didn't make any effort to contradict him. He was not usually a vicious person. He also wasn't someone who gave a damn about what other people did with their lives. He wanted everyone to be happy with their own decisions. He just wanted to be left alone to live the life he knew was right for him.

However, he never actually apologized.

For days afterward, he questioned what made him lose his cool. It wasn't just being yelled at and unfairly judged. Did he subconsciously feel there was some truth to Sue's argument? Did he actually feel some doubts about the decisions he'd made for how to live his life?

He wasn't sure. But either way, he felt as strong as ever that breaking up with Rebecca was the right thing. He could feel the last drops of passion draining out of their love. Stupid little tiffs were now a standard feature of their every interaction. They had settled into a life more routine than he could bear. And he did not want kids. He was sure of that. *If everyone who didn't want to be a father was as mature and responsible as me,* he thought, *there would be a lot fewer messed up kids in the world.*

*Endings are not inherently a bad thing,* he thought. *They often lead to new beginnings.*

Endings. His life had already featured so many even though he was only in his mid-thirties. And those endings were likely the real reason behind his and Sue's rift.

They had lost both their parents at an early age. Their father had a heart attack. Their mother was tragically killed during a robbery at a convenience store. Both events happened within a year and a half of each other.

For some siblings, horrific losses of this sort would bring them closer together. But for some reason, these tragedies isolated Dan and Sue.

It probably stemmed from their personalities. Both of the McCoy siblings were naturally strong and independent. Initially, in the face of death all around them, the only way they could each, respectively, keep from slipping into hopelessness was to forge a personal fortress of self-sustainment.

Some would say Dan hardened to the world. Dan would say that he became more resilient. It took a long time to move past his parents' deaths. It would be inaccurate to say that he ever got over them. But he did feel that facing tragedy at such a young age granted him a sense of perspective for the life ahead that those who had never dealt with loss sorely lacked.

Dan never got upset about the petty insignificant worries which marred most people's daily existences. He was unperturbed when the car wouldn't start or when the cable went out or when he lost his footing while surfing and sprained or broke his arm.

He did not get annoyed when friends questioned him time and time again as to whether he was against the idea of a permanent relationship because of a fear of loss. A fear that they believed stemmed from his parents' deaths. He wasn't afraid of loss. Far from it. He had lived with true loss and it prepared him to deal with life's far less severe, regular, necessary endings. This was why he had no problem saying goodbye to relationships he had enjoyed at one time when things had run their natural course. Because he knew he could be okay alone.

Sue was similarly untroubled by life's accumulating annoyances. She similarly felt that she needed nothing and no one else to survive. But she also saw creating a family as the purest *good* one could accomplish in the fickle and often crushing universe.

For years and years Dan and Sue didn't particularly clash, but they also never bonded. They spoke occasionally. They spent holidays together cordially. And they were united by their adoration of their younger sister Holly.

Holly was very different from her older siblings. While Dan and Sue were easygoing and subdued, Holly was bubbly and energetic. While Dan and Sue were mostly creatures of introspection and solitude, prone to hiding their inner world from even those they were closest to, Holly was an expanse of extroversion. She was never to be found apart from at least ten of her closest friends and she was known to express her feelings with endearingly alarming openness.

Perhaps Holly had been too young when her parents had died to be affected in the same manner as Dan and Sue. Perhaps all of their personalities were there from birth and would have emerged eventually regardless of their childhood veering wildly off course. Either way, one fact was certain: Holly was the primary emotional link between Dan and Sue. They both loved her in a way they never did each other.

Then, three and a half years ago, tragedy struck again. Holly was diagnosed with pancreatic cancer. She died eight months later.

Holly's death was even more devastating than their parents' had been. The universe's callous disposal of someone so young and beloved was completely unreasonable to both of the remaining McCoy children.

In a way though, they had been preparing their whole life for further anguish. They were equipped to coldly march through the immediate shock and oppressive silence a loved one's removal leaves hanging in the air, because they had already shielded themselves against the harsh world long ago. It didn't mean they were any less sad. It just meant that they didn't face the usual pain of trying to fruitlessly rebel against a horrible situation. They were as accepting as anyone can be in those circumstances.

Though they kept in touch for some time after Holly's funeral, there was no doubt that their sister's death severely damaged their relationship. Holly had been the bridge between them and without her, they were inaccessible to each other, stranded on opposing sides of the emotional river.

In truth, Dan knew Holly's death was the real reason that he and Sue didn't speak anymore. But their subtle rift had needed an actual argument to bring about an incommunicative grudge. His breakup with Rebecca had been just the occasion to bring the inevitable into fruition.

Now, two years in, Dan was tired of holding a grudge. He was tired of not speaking to his sister.

But today was not the day the silence would end.

*Maybe I'll call her sometime soon*, he thought to himself again.

*Maybe.*

Suddenly, Dan remembered the actual reason he had taken out his calendar. To pencil in the conference he had just been asked to conduct. He flipped to the May 28th page and excitedly jotted down "Marriott Hotel, 11 a.m. presentation."

Dan shook off the sadness that thoughts of his sister had generated by remembering how well his career had been going lately.

Just a year and half earlier going out on his own had seemed like a major gamble. Now, it was paying off and seemed like the smartest move he could have made.

Dan worked as a financial advisor. For years he had been an employee of a large firm, forced to toe the company line, push investments his bosses suggested he push, and place a corporate agenda above the particular needs of his individual clients.

Eventually, he had just about as much as he could stomach of that kind of life and he struck out into the world as a unit of one. Almost everyone he knew said it was a bad idea and there had certainly been a scary patch at the start, but eventually word of his unique, honest, helpful brand of advice spread.

In three years he went from being a complete nobody in the industry to a man with his own nationally broadcast radio show.

He loved it. He loved what he did. He loved helping people with their finances in a real direct way and receiving recognition for his work. He didn't think it was too arrogant to find enjoyment in praise.

And yet, at this moment, his mind awash with thoughts of Sue and Rebecca and the past he did his best to ignore, he didn't feel all that wonderful.

He felt a very unusual jolt of emptiness and suddenly was overcome with a desire to hold a woman in his arms. For a brief minute Dan wanted the comforting heat of another human being so bad that it almost made him choke.

He stood up and hurriedly stepped outside into the ever perfect San Diego air. He closed his eyes. He let all his thoughts float out of his mind. *I like to be alone*, he reminded himself. It was no lie. Dan felt great satisfaction in solitude. Even when he was in a relationship he needed a significant amount of alone time to feel at peace.

*I like to be alone*, he repeated. Why did the truth sometimes feel so... incomplete?

# PART I:
## MAY 2013

# 1

Kara was in the process of answering Tony's question about her very large family when he interrupted her to flag down the waitress for more breadsticks.

Tony was thirty-eight. Divorced. A bit pudgy. A bit balding. And one of the most appealing men who had messaged her on Match.com thus far.

Kara had joined the online matchmaking service a month earlier. She was convinced by the urging of perfect looking television promo couples who claimed they weren't actors and had really found each other on the website. (Though they very well could have found each other on Match AND been actors. One couldn't sneeze in Los Angeles without interrupting someone getting ready for "the most important audition of their entire life.")

Several more attractive men than Tony had contacted Kara. But the messages they sent were so lewd, or dumb, or some offensive combination of both, that she would have given up and completely removed her account if she hadn't already made a down payment for three months on the site.

At their classiest, men would message her with unhelpfully simple greetings like: "Hey Baby, what's up?"

At their worst, they would send shockingly revolting statements along the lines of "I bet U screw like an animal."

Tony, on the other hand, had sent her a nice message asking about a book they had both read. He asked her out to dinner. He used proper grammar. This last fact was particularly important to Kara, as a current student of English. It was difficult enough to master a second language. It was even harder to try to understand butchered, slang versions of it.

Tony was far from her dream man. Unfortunately, the time for dreaming seemed long past.

Kara had just finished up her final year as a student at the University of Southern California. She had been living in California for four years on a student visa which was set to expire at the beginning of September. Despite America's reputation as a nation of immigrants, the prospect of getting a foothold on the path to citizenship was rather difficult. If things didn't change dramatically in the next four months, Kara would be forced to return home to Mexico.

Kara had heard rumors of a green card lottery, which had given her hope of receiving some sort of destined chance to remain in the country. But when she finally looked into the details of the lottery she had so excitedly been telling her family about for three and a half years, she found out with breath depleting disappointment that she was not actually eligible. The "Diversity Immigrant Visa Program" as the U.S. Citizenship and Immigration Services referred to it, was a lottery only available to people coming from countries with particularly low rates of immigration to the United States. Mexico was not on this list and almost certainly never would be again.

So, if Kara wanted to stay in America she had two real options. She could try to somehow obtain a position of employment that would grant her a green card (Her research showed this was going to be difficult with her limited qualifications). Or she could marry an American. There was also the option of remaining illegally but Kara was too much of a rule follower to ever consider this option widely used by many of her countrymen.

As the days went by, a clock ticked ever onward inside her mind, constantly reminding her that her Visa's expiration was fast approaching, and it was time for her to do something about it.

At the moment, Kara didn't want to think about her visa troubles. She wanted to relax and enjoy her date. She didn't want to spend the whole evening analyzing Tony's physical features and she definitely didn't want to judge his minute by minute social behavior against some made up scale of acceptable husband quality.

Yet she also couldn't help but judge him for his excessive consumption of breadsticks.

"Sorry. You were saying?" said Tony, officially declaring that his interruption was over.

"Right," she said. "I am the youngest of three. This is small for my family. I have my older brother Ricardo and older sister Carmen. My father is one of six children and my mother is one of eight. I have twenty seven first cousins."

"That's a lot of cousins," said Tony, chomping into a breadstick and chewing with his mouth wide open. "What's that like?"

*Overwhelming and wonderful,* thought Kara. Though she lacked to English skills to properly express the complicated sentiment. She actually had a trip home scheduled for the coming weekend. Just speaking of her family filled her with both incredible love and tremendous dread. There was an ever-comforting warmth provided by her brood's unfiltered affection. But there was also tension. Having to answer questions about her marriage prospects and potential future babies to twenty plus drinking Tijuanans was sometimes enough to make her want to run to the desert and bury herself in the sand.

"It's nice," she answered.

"Do they all live in the same house?"

"What?"

"I've heard it's a bit overcrowded down there."

"No," she said, mildly insulted. "Each family has its own house."

"Sorry," he said, drowning his breadstick in marinara sauce. "I didn't mean anything. I was just…trying to make conversation."

"Do you want to hear a joke?" inquired Tony. He hoped to regain some ground through the magic of laughter.

"Okay," said Kara.

"What do you call a fly with no wings?"

"What?"

"A walk."

Kara stared at Tony. She waited for the punchline.

"Because he can't fly," explained Tony.

"Oh. This is the joke?"

"Yeah, that's the joke."

"Oh."

"Sorry. My daughter used to love that one."

"You have a daughter?"

"Uh. Yeah. Did I not mention that?"

"No."

"Oops. Yeah, I have a twelve year old girl. Michelle."

Tony took out his wallet and showed Kara a picture.

"She is beautiful," said Kara.

"Thanks."

Kara felt a sudden surge of jealousy towards this man who, moments before, she pitied for his terrible joke telling and his sloppy eating habits. Kara's biological clock had hardly reached its expiration date; she was only twenty-four. Nevertheless, the inner sense that she already was a mother, who had merely yet to produce a child, grew exponentially larger by the day. Sometimes, when she was supposed to be paying attention in class, or when she was working her job as an in-home nurse, her thoughts drifted away from her and entered the atmosphere of motherhood fantasies. In these day dreams, she clutched a child and felt the most monumental bliss she had ever felt in her life.

"What is it like?" she asked.

"What?" said Tony.

"To have a daughter."

"Oh," he said. "It's the most wonderful thing in the world."

Kara said a polite good night to Tony when he dropped her off at her apartment building. She nodded halfheartedly when he suggested they might get together again and leaned in for an awkward hug. He was a sweet man, and she felt slightly bad for so wholeheartedly rejecting him. She was anxious to return home and wash off the uncomfortable feeling of a date that fell way below her romantic expectations.

Entering her apartment, she was greeted with giddy affection by her dog Ricki, a tiny Maltese with a boatload of spirit. She scooped Ricki up into her hands and was comforted by her licks.

Eventually Kara placed Ricki down, went to her bedroom, and started to pack her suitcase for her trip back to Tijuana. As she packed, her thoughts circled repetitively on the details of her frustrating situation.

It wasn't that Kara really expected to meet Prince Charming. It was just that she really really wanted to. Wants and expectations often exist side-by-side as strange bedfellows.

It made it very difficult to go on first dates when her mind was filled with such soaring hopes. She scanned the listings of Match.com like the aisles of the grocery store, searching for the best deal. It was impossible to relax and enjoy herself when she was worried that she might end up with less than she emotionally wanted on one hand and with less than she practically needed on the other. She wanted a powerful man to love her and kiss and her and hold her tight. And she wanted someone nearby who would fall in love with her immediately and give her children and marry her so she could stay in America.

It had not always been Kara's intention to remain in the U.S. permanently. She wasn't sure if it was even her intention now. Yet there were multiple factors which made getting a green card seem appealing, if not essential.

Kara had fallen in love with the U.S., she had to admit to herself, though it made her feel somewhat guilty. It wasn't the scale of living, though the wide spread of affluence was noticeable. It was something less tangible. It was a sense of hope and possibility that existed among the citizens. If she had to generalize, she would say that Mexicans were, by and large, more enthusiastic and joyful than most Americans. But Americans had a much stronger sense of optimism. When an American had an aspiration, he could work towards it and really believe that it was going to happen. She liked being in America because here she felt like her story was leading somewhere. In Mexico, she had been always been happy. But she had felt as if there was no story at all. Just day to day existence.

Still, her desire to remain in the States was far from completely selfish. She had been sending a great portion of the money she had been making back home to her family. For the past two years she had worked as a day nurse for a sweet, but chronically silent, old woman named Evelyn. Every time she received a pay check from the nursing service which hired her she immediately cashed it and put seventy-five percent of her earnings in an envelope for her parents. She sent this money to her mother Maria, who somehow had kept these donations secret from her father Juan. Maria seemed to think that her stubborn husband would refuse to accept financial help from someone of the younger generation. Either way, Kara was aware that her contributions meant a great deal to her family and that she could never make the same kind of money in Mexico, where she had brought in minimal wages as a hairdresser before she had started school in the states. The same job opportunities simply didn't exist there.

Kara plunged her hand into the bottom of her sock drawer and pulled out the envelope of cash which was her latest contribution to her family. She tucked it deep into her suitcase.

Fully packed, she zipped up her belongings.

"Home," she said out loud, using the English word. She thought about the term and its meaning.

Kara had been in the United States of America for four years and it suddenly occurred to her that Tijuana no longer felt like home. Sure, it would always be where she grew up and where her family lived. And she would always love it for the deep emotional connections it held. But Los Angeles was now her home. America was her home. And yet, it also wasn't.

When Kara thought of the word "home," what she really thought of was love. She thought, *I will never really have a home until I have someone to love.*

The moment the door opened, Kara was consumed by an aggressive array of hugs so intense she had trouble breathing. She dropped her suitcase to the ground and barely hung on to the collar with which she led Ricki.

Her cousins Adriana, Martha, and Margarita, as well as her sister Carmen all attacked her with suffocating affection. They had spotted her approach from the window.

"Kara's here!" they yelled with glee, as the house full of family applauded.

"Hi!" Kara said through laughter, unable to hug back because her arms were completely locked to her sides by the surrounding bodies.

When the assault of love finally ended, Adriana and Margarita snatched up Ricki and Kara got the chance to give her sister an individual hug.

"Hello big sister," she said.

"I am so happy to see you," said Carmen. "Now someone else can hold my child all night."

Carmen reached into the hands of her husband Jorge, who approached to give his own greeting, and plucked out her sleeping six month old Isabella. She plopped the infant in Kara's arms so suddenly that she almost slipped through Kara's hands and fell to the floor.

"God, be careful!" said Kara. "I almost dropped her."

"If you did, at least I would get some more sleep at night. Night after night of baby crying is enough to drive anyone crazy," said Carmen.

Kara shook her head at her sister's twisted sense of humor and looked down at Isabella. The baby was intensely adorable. Perhaps, as Carmen said, she did not sleep at night, but she was sound asleep just then. Laying there with her eyes closed, Isabella was the picture of innocence. For a moment, Kara pretended that Isabella was her own child and felt a familiar wave of jealousy take hold.

"Okay, I miss her already," said Carmen. She grabbed Isabella from Kara's arms and gave her a big kiss. "Isn't she the most precious thing in the world?"

"She is," Kara agreed, as she hugged Jorge hello. "So where is the birthday boy?"

The party was a celebration for the birthday of Carmen's older child, Carlos, who was turning five. Carmen told Kara that Carlos was playing out back with the many other children, big and small, birthed in recent years by various family members. She led the way.

The house was packed in tight with Kara's relatives and the journey to the backyard was slow going. Every two feet they progressed, Kara was halted by another excited cousin or aunt or uncle who wanted to know all about living in America. She stopped to embrace her older brother Ricardo and his pregnant wife Louisa. She stopped to say hello to her grandmother Rosita who lectured her for bringing Ricki since "the thing probably has fleas." Each time they were hindered, Carmen shook her head in joking disapproval and said something along the lines of, "Now that you are an American, everyone treats you like a movie star."

Eventually they did make their way to Carlos, who kicked around a soccer ball with his older cousins Ian and Luis. Also with them was Kara's mother, Maria.

She kneeled down and said hello to Carlos, who was too busy impressing his friends with his goal kicking skills to give her more than a quick pat on the back. Then she turned to her mom.

"Where is papa?" she asked, after a long hug.

"Still working," said Maria.

"Ay, Mama. Did he tell them it was his grandson's birthday?"

"It is not good to make special requests to these men. They might not give you the work next time. You know how these construction jobs are."

"How is his back?"

"I think he is in great pain but he will not admit it to me. He gets annoyed anytime I ask."

"He cannot keep working like this. His body is going to give out at some point."

"I know honey, I know. He is stubborn your father. And the truth is, we still need the money."

"I'm giving you money," said Kara, lowering her voice. "I brought more with me today."

"I know. And I am grateful."

"Why can't I tell papa? Maybe if I tell him he won't feel the need to work so hard."

"We've been over this. All telling your father will do is make him refuse to accept any more donations from his daughter. Like I said, he is a stubborn man."

"If you say so."

"Don't worry about your father. I'm just glad you're doing so well back in the States. I'm very proud of you Kara."

"Thanks, mama."


The party was a blast. Though Southern California had its share of Mexican cuisine to offer, it wasn't the same as the dishes Kara could find back home. She gorged herself on corn tortilla tacos and chile con carne and all manner of homemade dishes, feeling memories of her youth flood back with every high flavored bite. As everyone ate, the children raucously played and Kara laughed and chatted with all her relatives. She was so happy to see everyone, even if their view of her as some sort of bastion of societal advancement seemed a bit unfounded.

Eventually Carlos decided he'd had enough of the preliminary birthday activities. He ceased all other action and told each and every party attendant that he was ready for his cake and would not wait for it one more minute.

The adults could hardly resist his charms. Maria prepared the candles and the other children swooned with envy as the sugary iced display was placed in front of the birthday boy, aflame with the burning candles of another passed year.

It was never easy to bring movement and speech to a halt in a room of thirty half-drunk Tijuanans, but Carmen's angry glares managed to quiet the buzz to an acceptable level for Carlos to make his wish. He blew out the candles and was serenaded with a booming rendition of "Feliz Cumpleanos para ti." Of course, what he really wanted was the cake itself, and as soon as Maria cut him the first slice, he stuffed it in his face like a long starved animal. Rosita shook her head in disapproval, but Maria and Carmen merely laughed at the icing which now obscured the boy's delighted face.

Lost in the shuffle of the official birthday ceremony was Kara's father's return to his own home. He snuck past Kara and the others, who gleefully watched Carlos stuff his face, and walked up to the boy of honor.

"Care to share some of that cake with your Abuelo?" said Juan.

Kara was delighted by the long delayed appearance of her father. She rushed over to him.

"Papa!" she declared as she threw her arms around him.

"Careful Kara," said Carmen. "You might break him."

"I'm stronger than I've ever been," insisted Juan.

"Where have you been?" asked Kara. "Mama said you were working on a job."

"I was providing for my family."

"You should be *enjoying* your family."

"I am now. It's great to see you Kara. How are you?"

"I'm just fine. Let's get you a piece of cake. You've been working hard all day. You deserve one."

"You spoil me," he said, smiling.

As far back as she could remember, Kara had always been incredibly close with her father. She had a great relationship with her mother too, but it wasn't the like the wordless, soul-sparking, pillar of connection that existed between her and Juan. They were each other's main source of strength in a way – even when they went months without talking. In fact, they never talked all that much. Not even when they saw each other. Juan was a man of few words. He spoke only as much as necessary. This prevented some from ever becoming too close to Juan. But not Kara. She loved him with all that she was. All her young life he had protected her. Now he was getting older and Kara felt it was her turn to take charge. It was her turn to take care of her beloved father.

After the dust settled and Kara said goodbye to each of her relatives and helped her family clean the house from the mess created by the party, she cradled Ricki in her arms and retreated to her childhood bedroom for a moment of rest on her old bed.

Her moment of seclusion did not last long. Carmen peeked her head into the room and, spotting her sister, plopped herself on the bed.

"So…now that we have a moment alone you can really tell me about your life in America."

"What do you mean?"

"I want to hear the good stuff."

"What good stuff?"

"How's your sex life?"

"Carmen!"

"Oh, don't pretend you're the Mother Mary. I'm married and you're still single. I have to live vicariously through you now. So let me hear some stories!"

"There's nothing to tell."

"Sure there is. You're a beautiful Mexican girl. I bet the gringos are fighting each other off to get in your pants."

"You would be disappointed."

"None of those college boys have gone after you at their parties?"

"I don't go to college parties. They are like children, those boys."

"You're right. You've always been smart, my sister. You must be going after the older rich gringos. And they must be lining up for you."

"You watch too many movies Carmen," said Kara. "Anyway American men, they are so bland. So boring. They have no passion," she added unconvincingly in an effort to thwart her sister's efforts.

"Have you gone any dates, at least?"

"A few."

"And?"

"I don't know Carmen. I haven't found…what I'm looking for."

"What would that be?"

"I…I don't know."

Carmen sensed her sister suddenly get vulnerable and she pressed pause on her barrage of questions.

Kara turned her head away. She looked at Ricki, who she loved so much for her eternal innocence. She pet her.

"You're not the only girl who wants to find true love," Carmen finally said. "But finding a nice rich gringo to marry you wouldn't be half bad. Make a good life for yourself! You have that chance. You should take it. Or at least have some fun! You're only young once!"

"Okay," said Kara.

Another long moment passed. When Carmen spoke again, her tone was quite different. Her usual fiery delivery was greatly subdued.

"Look. I know we have never talked about these things. I figure that you probably used to talk to Teresa about boys."

Kara turned her head away from her sister. She felt tears well up at the mere mention of Teresa's name.

Teresa had been Kara's best friend all of her life. Since she was two years old. She had died on a trip with her family to Mexico City four years before. Just before Kara left for the States. Teresa had gotten caught up in the crossfire of a drug related shooting. Her mother was also hit but she survived. Teresa was not as lucky.

Kara had a lot of trouble making friends these days. Every time she chatted briefly with someone new, she thought of Teresa and how much she missed her. New friendship made her think of her old friendship, so she avoided it. She supposed in some ways, her reluctance to return to Mexico was also because of Teresa. She didn't want to live in a place that would remind her so much of the past and loss. She wanted to press forward into new hopeful beginnings.

Kara tried not to think about her old friend too much because of the immense pain every memory of Teresa gave her. But she was always there, at the back of every lonely life moment.

"I want you to know that I'm your sister and you can tell me anything," Carmen continued. "Everyone needs to have someone they can talk to. I'm always here for you."

Kara looked up at her sister. She felt the most intense love for her.

"Thanks Carmen," she said.

Carmen put her hand on Kara's.

"Now go back to the States and get laid!" said Carmen.

There was a two second silence and then both of the Gomez sisters burst out laughing. Kara fell back on the bed, unable to control her chuckles for several wonderful minutes.

The rest of the weekend was quite enjoyable, though Kara was ready to return to her new life in Los Angeles. She was concerned that too much time spent lounging in the comforts of her old home would make her forget what she really wanted.

As she packed, Juan entered her room to talk to her.

"Is anything the matter my dear?" he asked.

One of the disadvantages to a having a connection with someone which needed no words, was that they could sometimes read your mind when you had no desire to communicate your mental state with them.

"No. I'm fine," she said. "Why?"

"You seem a little off."

She was about to lie – say that she had a cold or something – but the effort of misleading her father was much greater than it was with most people, and she was already using most of her reserved energy to keep the secret of the money she was giving Maria.

"I'm just…feeling uncertain about my future," she admitted.

"I see."

"I am waiting for things to happen, but sometimes I do not feel very patient."

"Perhaps you should not wait then."

"What do you mean?"

"You have to go out and make what you want happen. Kara, you have an opportunity that no one in our family has ever had. You should take it."

Kara felt a mixture of guilt and pride. Guilt, because her father had spent most of his life doing grueling physical labor, as had most of his relatives before him, and she had already lived a more charmed life than he ever had. Pride, because her father remained strong throughout every harshness life had to offer and she knew, as his child, she had the same strength residing inside her.

"You can do anything you want Kara. I have faith in you. You just need to work to make it happen," said Juan.

Kara ran over to Juan and hugged him tight.

"I love you papa," she said.

Juan was right. She could not wait for life to happen to her. She had to go out and make it happen.

# 2

Kara was dressed in her scrubs and about to leave for work when her phone rang. It was her boss, Patricia.

"Kara, hi," she said. "Did you leave for Evelyn's yet?"

"No," said Kara. "I was just about to."

"Okay, good. Ashley just called me. Evelyn passed last night."

"Oh. I am sorry to hear that. She was a nice lady."

Kara meant it. Evelyn had been quite kind to her in the two years that she had worked as her nurse, even if she didn't speak much. News of her death was not precisely a surprise. Evelyn was ninety-three and increasingly prone to bouts of sickness. The end of human life was never pleasant, but Kara figured she better get used to it if she wanted this to be her permanent profession. A few hours difference and it would have been her who discovered the body.

"It's always the hardest part of the job," said Patricia. "Watching people leave this world for the next."

"Yeah."

"But listen. Would you mind still working today? One of my other nurses called out and I need someone to take her shift."

"Yes. Of course. I would like to work."

"Great. Do you have a pen handy?"

When she pulled up, Kara double checked the address to make sure she hadn't made some mistake.

The abode in front of her was more palace than house. At least in Kara's personal scale of living perception. She could have fit at least three duplicates of the house she grew up in inside of Evelyn's home, and the residence in front of her dwarfed that dwelling by a significant degree.

The numbers all checked out so Kara parked her car and proceeded to the front door.

The night nurse responded to the doorbell and let Kara in.

"You must be Kara," she said. "Come on in."

"Hi, nice to meet you," said Kara.

"I'm Dee. Ramon is upstairs. Come on up. I'll introduce you."

As Dee led her through the halls, Kara tried to use her peripheral vision to take in the mansion without overtly gawking.

Each room was more striking than the next. Shelves were filled to the ceiling with books in one room, the walls were filled ten feet wide with sculptures in another. Yet the place was far from garish. It was decorated with tradition and class. There was also a definite Mexican flair to the schemes. The cultural familiarity put Kara a little more at ease in the midst of such wealth.

Most impressive of all were the photographs. All around the house were images of an imposing businessman (presumably Ramon), over the course of fifty years, meeting and shaking hands with various important looking politicians, dignitaries, and CEOs, as well as accepting awards and delivering speeches to captivated crowds. There was a noticeable lack of family photographs. Though Kara did notice one portrait of Ramon standing with a younger, handsome male who bore a strong resemblance to the images of Ramon in his youth.

Finally they made it to the bedroom. Kara followed Dee in.

The room was massive. It looked like someone had put a bed in a cathedral. The king size mattress was topped by a regal canopy and all around were artworks that might have been stolen from the Vatican.

Propped up with pillows on the bed, reading the Wall Street Journal, was the man from the photos.

"Ramon, I'd like you to meet Kara," said Dee. "She's going to be your day nurse today."

"A pleasure to meet you Kara," he said, then promptly returned to reading his paper.

Dee glared at him suspiciously, as if not trusting his politeness.

"I will see you tonight Ramon."

"See you tonight," he said.

Dee motioned to Kara to follow her into the hall. She gave Kara a thorough run down of Ramon's prescriptions and medical requirements.

"Thanks," said Kara. "Anything else?"

"Yes. Try not to be offended by Mr. Salazar. He's got a mouth on him."

"A mouth?" Kara was not familiar with the expression.

"You'll see," said Dee with a grin. "Take it easy Kara."

"You too. Bye."

Kara went back into Ramon's bedroom, where he promptly threw down his newspaper.

"Hello again," she said.

"So you're the new day nurse?" he said.

"Just for today, I think, Mr. Salazar."

"Please. Call me Ramon. I hope it is for more than just today. You must thank your boss for me."

"Yes. Of course. What am I thanking her for?"

"For finally sending me a nurse who's actually pretty!"

Kara blushed.

"Oh. Well…" She was unsure how to respond.

"It's so boring in here all day," he continued. "It's nice to have some eye candy to look at for a change." He laughed in a way that indicated he wished for Kara to laugh with him. She produced a little fake chuckle, though in truth she felt somewhat uncomfortable.

"So," she said, wishing to change the subject. "It's breakfast time. Should I prepare you some food?"

"There are several containers of fruit in the refrigerator. It would be wonderful if you would make me a fruit salad."

"Okay. I shall go get the fruit salad ready," she said, thinking foolishly that she had succeeded in moving on to topics that did not involve her appearance.

"Be quick about it!" said Ramon. "I like looking at you more than I like looking at the Wall Street Journal."

Kara's hopeful smile drooped.

"Be right back," she said.

As she walked out of the room she heard Ramon bellow, "And I love the Wall Street Journal! It's really informative!"

Kara prayed to God while she mixed blueberries, grapes, pineapple, and peach into a proper breakfast fruit concoction. She asked for patience in dealing with the lecherous old man in her care.

When she walked back into his room and presented him with the bowl on his tray table he said, "You look delicious!"

Kara thought that was well over the line of acceptability and if she didn't speak up now she would be forced into tolerating this lewdness the entire rest of the day.

"Mr. Salazar—"

"Ramon. Please. Ramon."

"Fine. Ramon. That language is NOT appropriate."

"What language?" he said. "Oh! You thought I was talking to you! I was talking to my fruit salad!"

Kara rolled her eyes with force to indicate how little truth she thought his statement contained.

"Thank you for the fruit salad," he said.

"You are welcome," she said.

Kara did her best to avoid Ramon's peering eyes the rest of the day. She took it upon herself to clean three of the house's bathrooms, as well as part of the kitchen.

When she did see him again, to bring him his midday pills, he was watching the Financial News Network on TV.

"Time for your pills Mr— Ramon," she said.

He muted the TV and turned to her seriously.

"Kara, can I ask you a question?"

"Yes."

"If I take my pills, will you give me a kiss on the cheek?"

Kara broke out her eye roll again. Her eyes were getting plenty of exercise on this day of work. She unsnapped the Monday section of his pill organizer.

"Just one little kiss?"

Embarrassed and exasperated, Kara thrust the pill organizer into his lap. She forcefully placed a glass of water on his night table and turned to carry herself out of the room.

"It's okay," he said as she exited. "You can think about it. You don't have to decide right away!"

Back at her apartment that night, Kara's cell phone rang. It was Patricia.

"Well I don't know what you did today," she said, "but the client is absolutely raving about you. He insists on having you as his permanent day nurse."

Kara groaned.

"What was that?" asked Patricia.

"Nothing," said Kara.

"As it turns out, I was going to ask you to keep working for him anyway. The girl who had been in that slot apparently won't be able to work again for a while. But lucky for us, he doesn't know that and has offered extra money to have you in the position."

"I see," said Kara.

Kara searched her mind for a reason to turn down the job but she couldn't find one that would justify doing so. The woman formerly in her care had died and there was no guarantee she would immediately be placed back with a client. Plus, she had no business refusing extra income that her family desperately needed; particularly with her visa expiration looming and the chance that soon enough she wouldn't be able to work in the United States at all. Her words of reservation about Ramon lingered in her throat, unspoken.

"You'll officially start tomorrow," said Evelyn.

Kara braced herself for the onslaught of harassment when she said hello to Ramon the next morning.

She was surprised to be greeted instead with a rather tame, "Good morning Kara."

Ramon was busy fumbling about in his closet.

"Were going out today," he said. "I have to find something nice to wear. We can't have it said that I've lost my sense of style in my old age."

"Oh," she said. "Where are we going?"

"It's a financial conference. Likely nothing that will interest you. I apologize in advance."

*Well at least you apologize for something*, she thought.

"I would love another fruit salad, my dear," he said. "One can't start the day without a healthy meal."

Again, Kara lingered in the room, waiting for the uncomfortable sexual fawning. Nothing came.

Pleased, she turned to walk out.

"Of course…" he said, interrupting her departure.

"Yes?"

"No fruit you gather will please me more than those melons you're walking around with."

Disgusted, she whipped around and stormed out of the room.

An hour later Kara and Ramon's driver, a middle aged man named Paul, helped Ramon into the backseat of Paul's black Lincoln sedan. Paul folded up Ramon's wheelchair and loaded it into the trunk. Ramon said he could walk without it, but the going would be significantly slower and the day would last significantly shorter.

Paul drove them to the Marriott Hotel, in the heart of downtown Los Angeles. After fighting an hour and a half of traffic to go eleven miles, they finally arrived at their destination.

There they promptly unloaded the wheelchair and Ramon plopped himself in it. They said goodbye to Paul, who would pick them up when the event was over, and Kara wheeled Ramon into the lobby.

Kara was quite surprised by the size of the crowd. Throughout the lobby, folks were hustling and bustling and chatting. There must have been close to two hundred people. She could smell the excited anticipation floating just above the hotel's intentionally projected vanilla scent.

"What's all the commotion about?" Kara asked.

"It's all about him," said Ramon.

He pointed towards a poster for the day's event. On it was a photograph of Dan McCoy. It read: "Dan McCoy. Host of "The Soul Investor Radio Show'. Appearing in Ballroom A on May 28th at 11 a.m."

Kara couldn't help but notice how handsome the man on the poster was, with his muscular physique and his boyish sandy blonde hair.

"Who is he?" she asked.

"I think he's the best investment and finance expert in California, which would make him the best on the west coast, and one of the best in the country. He's already made me a lot of money."

"You know him?"

"Not personally. He has a website and a radio show where he gives tips. He really knows what he's talking about. Anyway, we're going to see him today. Again, I'm sorry if it's boring to you. My nephew Raul was supposed to take me but he had to cancel."

"I don't mind," said Kara, a bit too eagerly. "I look forward to it!"

"Well good. You might learn something from him. I think this McCoy is the smartest up and comer around when it comes to business and money. Even if he is a gringo!" Ramon laughed.

His derogatory joke didn't make much sense considering all of the photos he had of himself with caucasians in the house, but Kara fake chuckled in response anyway. In truth, she was more intrigued by Dan's good looks than his investment knowledge. Though she certainly had no intention of correcting Ramon.

"Well, wheel me in there," he said. "I want a good view!"

They settled just off center in the front row of the ballroom's folding chair auditorium. About twenty minutes later, the rest of the seats were filled and the lights dimmed to indicate the day was to begin.

Music played and out walked Dan McCoy onto the stage, dressed casually in jeans and a collared shirt with no tie. On its own, his outfit looked more like something someone would wear for drinks after work than to host a conference filled with businessmen in suits. But the way Dan wore it radiated confidence. There was an unsaid indication in his demeanor that the clothes mattered far less than who was wearing them.

After the applause died down, Dan began to speak.

"Thank you. Thank you very much. It's good to be here today. I value your time so I'm going to cut right to the chase. Most people working on Wall Street – whether they are investment bankers, hedge fund managers, investment advisors, or anyone in any other significant capacity within the finance industry – these people WANT – YOU – TO – BE – SCARED. They want you to think that without them, it's impossible to succeed."

Kara looked around the room. The same group of people who moments before had chatted in the lobby with a manic intensity, sounding like warring hives of insects trying to best one another's noise level, were silent, focused, and completely rapt in their attention.

She didn't blame them. Dan exuded charisma. His voice was magnetic. He had barely said anything and certainly nothing of any significance to her, yet she felt prepared to listen to him talk for days on end.

"Look, I understand we live in uncertain times," Dan continued, "However, this game of investing, this game of trading, has very little to do with intellect. And it has everything to do with *emotion*. If you can first learn the basics, and then learn to control your emotions, I will show you tools today that will significantly increase your odds of being a successful trader and a successful investor. My goal is not to have you get rid of your advisor. That's your choice. Instead, my goal is to get you to be on the same level as your advisor. To get them not to be your pilot, but your *co-pilot*."

Dan paused for a round of applause.

"If you listen to my radio show, you hear me say at the close of every show that no one – NO ONE – will watch and protect your money better than you. But I can help. And today I will help. I want to help you so that going forward you will sleep better knowing that from now on it is YOU who are in control."

The applause resumed, louder than ever. Dan gave off a slight smile of recognition that Kara only spotted because of her proximity to him. At the same moment his eyes, by chance, fell on her. Kara's heart went thundering.

His eyes moved on just as quickly as they landed on her, but not before Kara joined in the applause enthusiastically. Perhaps a little too enthusiastically. Ramon glanced over at her, looking confused.

"Just being polite," she said.

Dan waved his hands, asking for quiet. The crowd obliged.

"Now," he said. "Shall we begin?"

When he finished an hour and half later, Kara leapt up to give a standing ovation and Dan's eyes once again met her own. She knew it made little sense, but she felt a real connection. She felt that she was *meant* to be in this ballroom on this day. She felt suddenly very grateful towards Ramon for bringing her here. She looked down at him, smiling. He looked at her with complete puzzlement.

"Did you enjoy it *that* much?" he asked.

"Yes!" she said.

"Did you just like it because he is good looking?" he asked, on target.

"What? Uh…" she said, then finally after too much delay added, "Of course not."

"Riiiight. Alright time to go. Wheel me out of here."

Out in the lobby, Ramon halted Kara and said, "It's probably a good idea for me to use the men's room before we head back."

"Okay," said Kara. She started wheeling him in the men's room.

"Hold on Kara," he said. "I think I can handle this part myself."

"You sure you don't want my help in there?"

Ramon looked long at her, smirked, and laughed.

"Kara, if you don't want me to make inappropriate comments you really shouldn't set me right up for one."

"What?"

"Nevermind," he said. "I'll let you slide on this one. Yes, I'll be just fine in the bathroom. I'm old and weak but I'm not *that* old and weak."

"Okay," she said, still feeling extra tenderness towards the man for having brought her here today. "Well I'll be right out here if you need anything"

"Got it," he said, and went in to the Men's room.

Abruptly, waiting for Ramon to reemerge, Kara felt very anxious. Her sense of purpose floundered. How exactly was she supposed to meet this man she felt she had this unknown connection with? Maybe there was nothing meant to be about this particular afternoon at all. Maybe, as Ramon had implied, she had merely felt some infatuation for a handsome man and that's all there was to it. A cloud of discouragement floated over her. Her excitement dissipated.

But just as quickly, it returned.

For there in front of her was Dan. He walked down the hallway with a team of men. Calm, but commanding, he led the others. He was smiling brightly. Kara swooned, then panicked as he neared the front door of the building.

He was leaving. *It's now or never*, she thought.

Kara ran in front of Dan and his crew, stopping them in their tracks.

"I really enjoyed your talk today!" she said, much too loudly.

Various event attendees paused their own post-event conversations to glance over at the unusually loud woman and see why she was so loud.

Dan broke the tension by warmly approaching her. He extended his hand.

"Thank you very much, Miss…?"

"Kara. Kara Gomez."

She shook his hand.

"Very nice to meet you Miss Kara Gomez. I'm Dan McCoy."

After a moment, Dan chuckled.

"I'm going to need my hand back, Miss Gomez," he said.

Kara, in her daze, did not realize she had failed to remove her hand from the shake. Embarrassed, she quickly yanked it away.

"Sorry!" she said, again practically yelling for reasons she could not explain.

"Don't worry about it. So what brought you to the talk today?"

Kara noticed the impatient, inspecting eyes of Dan's associates. She almost ran off, right then and there, but she remembered the promise she made to herself – to not just stand back and wait for things to happen. She had to make them happen.

"Today, I brought a sick man to see you."

Dan looked confused. Kara quickly realized the other possible meaning of her statement and rephrased.

"That is, I am a nurse. Uh, my patient today, he was attending your talk and I was attending to him, so that is why I am here."

"I see. Well I'm glad you enjoyed it."

One of Dan's companions leaned towards him and said quietly, "Dan, we should really get going. We have a lot of ground to cover."

Kara swore she spotted a split second of annoyance on Dan's face. It quickly disappeared, replaced by his winning smile. "Okay," he said to the man, then turned back to Kara.

"I'm sorry. I gotta run. But here. Take my card. You can call me if you ever want to get together to talk…investment advice."

He handed her the card and their fingers brushed. Kara felt goose bumps emerge up and down her body.

"Okay. I will. Thank you," she said.

Dan rejoined his crew. He waved to her as they walked off.

"I heard yelling. Did I miss something exciting out here?" said Ramon, giving Kara a big jump as he suddenly appeared beside her.

"No. Nothing," she said through a smile. "Let's get you home."

# 3

Dan walked off the Marriott conference room stage and was thumped with excited pats on the back from Greg and Coady, the youthful duo who functioned as his tech crew.

"Thanks," said Dan. "How'd it go?"

"No problems with the live feed," said Coady.

"Great," said Dan. "Any numbers?"

"A hundred and thirty thousand hits."

Dan couldn't hold back a big grin of almost childlike wonder. "That's our best yet," in a voice that implied a calm adult reaction, though his real feeling was betrayed by the look on his face.

When Dan first started giving public lectures, he had thought it would be a beneficial idea to simultaneously broadcast his talks live on his website. He had no idea, however, just how large the audience would grow. At his last engagement, the online hits had for the first time eclipsed the ratings for his radio show. Now, today's numbers had blown the previous totals through the roof.

Dan suddenly realized his throat was completely parched. He had a habit of forgetting to drink in the middle of a talk. He became so wrapped in his performance and the captivated eyes in the audience that it slipped his mind. *Speaking of which, who was that girl in the front row?*, he thought. A beautiful

Hispanic woman had been sitting right up front, staring at him with a look of interest he could have sworn went beyond just learning new investment tricks.

He grabbed a bottle of water and took a much needed gulp.

He was about to ask Greg another question when he noticed both members of his crew looking at something behind him.

Dan turned around. At the doorway stood a man in a suit who Dan didn't recognize.

"Mr. McCoy, that was very impressive."

"Well thank you very much."

The man extended his hand.

"My name's Jim Roberts," he said. "I'm with The Financial Network."

Dan immediately shook but his hand but it took a moment for the level of his guest's importance to really sink in.

"It's great to meet you Jim," he said. Then added, "Can I get you a bottle of water of anything?" He realized the potential significance of the interaction and wanted to be hospitable.

"No I'm fine thanks. And the pleasure's all mine. That was some talk you gave today. Very impressive."

"Thanks. I appreciate that."

"Listen, are you hungry? I'd love to have some dinner and talk about possibly working together."

"That would be wonderful. I did actually tell my team I would take them out when we wrapped up here—"

"Bring them along," said Jim. He pulled out a business card and handed it to Dan. "I'm going to stop back in my room. Give me a call when you're all wrapped up here and I'll come down to meet you in the lobby."

"Great. Ten, fifteen minutes tops," said Dan.

When Jim left, Greg and Coady burst into simultaneous applause.

Dan smiled. "Alright. Alright. Calm down."

"The Financial Network. That's the big time," said Coady.

"They have deep pockets," said Greg. "I'm ordering a steak for dinner."

"I want a good impression here," said Dan. "You're ordering a salad."

Greg frowned. Coady laughed.

They packed up all of their equipment, loaded up the truck, and made their way to the lobby.

Dan was about to pull out Jim's card and call him up when Kara jumped in his path and yelled, "I really enjoyed your talk today!"

He recognized her immediately. She was the beautiful Hispanic girl he had spotted in the front row.

While they exchanged pleasantries, Dan looked into her eyes. He was certain that the reason she was speaking to him had nothing to do with financial advice. Dan had enough experience with women to recognize when someone was interested in him. Rarely, however, did a romantic opportunity storm up to him like a hungry animal starved for food.

As attractive as Kara was, Dan was more focused on his imminent meeting with Jim from the Financial Network. An opportunity for such a giant career leap occurred far less often than meeting a woman did.

Wishing to maintain his professional demeanor amongst his colleagues (not to mention the many onlookers in the lobby, all paying attention because of Kara's outrageous volume), he handed her his card, rather than asking for her number. He wasn't sure whether or not she would call, but he had a good feeling.

As they walked off and Dan pulled out Jim's card, Greg and Coady eyed Dan with smirks on their faces.

"What?" he said.

"I'm sure you're planning on giving that girl a nice long night of *financial advice*," said Greg.

After Paul dropped Kara and Ramon back at the Salazar estate, she helped Ramon slowly up the stairs and set him up to take a bath. This was no easy process and Ramon was notably quiet. Kara could see his physical strength drained from an atypically active day. She fully expected innuendo to pour out of his mouth as she helped undress him but the only thing he said was a quiet word of "Thanks."

While her employer soaked, she had some time to kill. So naturally she spent it replaying her interaction with Dan in her head hundreds of times. She wanted to see if she could unearth some detail of the scene which might indicate interest on Dan's part beyond just the desire for a new customer. She went back and forth. On one playback, she would be certain she remembered a glint in his eye which could mean nothing other than a deep immediate affection. On another recollection, the glint would disappear and she would be certain there was a subtle impatience in his voice, eager to be done with the interaction so he could back to the important things he had to do with his day.

Kara felt like she was back in high school, dishing with Teresa about some boy she had just spoken to in the lunch line. Except the boy was an incredibly successful grown man and Teresa was no longer here for her to speak to. She did feel a bit silly, fawning so much about a man she did not even know. But she couldn't help herself. Some irresistible cocktail had been mixed together in her mind between her ever increasing desire to find a man and her intense attraction to Dan. There were dangerous whispers of "destiny" steadily beating in her inner ear. She was well aware this line of thinking was unrealistic, but neither could she quiet the whispers.

Kara pulled out Dan's business card and wondered how long she had to wait before calling him was socially acceptable. She stared at it for a long minute, then convinced herself no waiting period was necessary. She would call him right now! Just as quickly she threw down her cell phone and reprimanded herself for being so swept up in her sudden crush that she would think an immediate phone call was okay. Then she sat still for a couple of minutes. Anxiety whooshed through her body, increasing in intensity like an avalanche. She picked up the business card again, certain she couldn't wait another minute, and began to dial. Then, she threw down her phone again before entering all the numbers, furious with herself over her lack of self-control. This process continued on a loop for about the next twenty five minutes. Finally, not because of any resolved decision – but rather because she accidentally dialed all of Dan's numbers and forgot to hang up before she heard ringing on the other end – she made the call.

Her heart beat hard as his phone rang…one…two…three…four times. She was just about to hang up and forget the whole thing when she heard a click and his voicemail message played.

"Hello, you have reached Dan McCoy of The Soul Investor, I am not available at the moment, please leave your name and number and a good time for me to get back to you."

Though she fully intended to start speaking immediately at the tone, Kara noticed that her vocal cords went completely inactive just when she most needed them. For ten seconds (an eternity on a voicemail) Kara said absolutely nothing. Just horrible, soul crushing silence.

Then, on second eleven, reaching down to some deep personal place of resolve, she forced herself to speak.

"Mr. McCoy, my name is Kara Gomez. We met at the hotel earlier today. And I just wanted to say that I liked your talk. And I liked meeting you too. And I would like to get some more of your…money wisdom…so, if you like, please call me. My number is 310-201-5543. Thanks and take care. Have a good night. Bye."

She hung up. It was not the most graceful of messages, she knew, and she was tempted to be mortified, but she actually felt optimistic. She felt hopeful he would call back soon.

Mainly, she felt relieved that she had made the call and the feeling of pressure was over.

She sat still for a minute, relaxed that the most nerve-racking part was over. She let her heart settle back into its normal rhythm.

Then, of course, she started to worry about when he would call back.

As it turned out, Greg was able to order his steak. He just had to eat it at a separate table.

When they entered the high end steak house where Jim suggested they eat, Jim politely asked Greg and Coady if they would mind sitting at a separate table so he and Dan could talk over business matters.

Greg was slightly perturbed by the request, but luckily Coady responded first. "Of, course we wouldn't mind," he said. In any case, Greg's feelings were eased when Jim insisted that they order anything on the menu they would like – an offer Greg had no issue accepting.

While they looked over the menu, Dan and Jim engaged in conversational warm up. They spoke of the difference of the weather in Southern California from Jim's home in New York and chit-chatted about other minor matters.

"Thanks again for getting dinner for my guys," Dan said, after they had told the waitress their orders.

"Don't worry about. I respect those who have loyalty to their people," said Jim.

"Loyalty is important. It's not something you can put a premium on."

"I'm glad you feel that way. Because that's exactly how we feel about our people at the Financial Network."

"Of course," said Dan.

"I'm going to get right to it Dan. We've been tracking your radio program and your website and, as I'm sure you know, today's talk, both in terms of streaming views on your site and radio listeners, was as at an all-time high. You broke all your previous records. You've got a small but loyal following Dan, and, what caught our eye, is that it's been growing exponentially over the past couple of years. To be frank, the network thinks you have the potential to be a breakout star next year.

"We would love to have you as a regular guest analyst on our channel.

We'd like to sign you for a twelve month period, with an option to extend. We can see how that goes and if you impress enough of the viewers and enough of the brass at the network, I wouldn't rule out the possibility of your own show some time in the future."

Jim paused for dramatic effect, so that his offer could sink in.

"Well Dan, how do you like the sound of that?" he asked.

Dan felt a surge of excitement ripple up and down his skin, such as he hadn't experienced in a long time. It felt like he had been piecing together a jigsaw puzzle for years, enjoying the leisure of it, never really expecting to finish, when suddenly, unexpectedly, the final piece was in his hand.

But Dan also wanted to be cautious. He took a deep breath and tried to rein in his emotions. The whole reason he had left his old employer and gone out on his own was so that he would not be beholden to any corporate overlord. He wanted to be free to actually help the common man; to speak the truth about financial matters and be accountable to no one but himself. He liked his independence. He knew it would be crazy to turn down an offer of this caliber to maintain autonomy, and he had no plans to, but he did need to make some things clear before he accepted.

"I like the sound of it a lot," said Dan. "But I do have one condition. I got to where I am by being direct. I think a thing – I say it. I say a thing – I mean it. I speak the truth, as I know it. I don't want to have to water down my style or tone. I don't like to be hemmed in by a lot of rules, so I'd like a lot of latitude on my appearances. Oh, also, I don't wear a tie. I just want to be upfront about that."

Jim did not respond for a moment. He took in Dan's statement. Then he smiled.

"I don't know that I would call that one condition. In truth Dan, that's asking a lot, but luckily, the whole reason we're interested in you is the no-nonsense approach you just displayed. It's why people like you and it's why, we think, our audience will like you. So I don't think your conditions will be a problem."

"The first conditions anyway," Jim added. "We'll see about that tie," he said with a laugh.

Dan laughed back. "I'm serious about the tie."

"Oh, I'm sure you are," said Jim. "So, just to be clear, you're going to accept our offer?"

"I am."

"Great. We'll email the papers. You can look them over, show them to your lawyer. Then, once we finalize everything, we'll get to work booking your first appearance."

Dan noticed his phone vibrating in his pocket. He ignored it completely, not wishing to show any rudeness to Jim.

"Sounds great," he said.


A half hour after leaving a message for Dan, Kara had received no response and felt suddenly certain that she never would.

Or, if he did call her back, it would just be about helping her with "money wisdom," as she had so stupidly phrased it. He was a handsome, successful, probably rich American. He could go out with any woman he liked. There was no reason he would have interest in a lowly immigrant nurse such as herself.

She did not feel stressed, however. She actually felt relaxed now that her geyser of hopes vanished. She felt foolish for having gotten caught up in a girlish crush for a man she knew nothing about. It was unlike her. She was the rational one in her family. Carmen was the daughter who fulfilled all of the stereotypes of fiery, emotional Mexican women. Kara had always been more practical. It was her level-headedness that allowed her to study in the States in the first place. She was able to focus and research opportunities and now she was able to make money for her family that they desperately needed.

Money which she would not be able to continue providing if she could not stay in America.

Which she probably would not be able to do unless she found a man.

And thus her circular thought process returned to its starting point and Kara's stress returned and she felt deeply sad. It was like she was moving through life in a dense, sticky fog, and she could not see the proper path to take. She was frustrated. She looked at her phone longingly and once more wished that Dan would call.

Just then, the doorbell rang.

The sound gave her a fright, locked as she was in her own thoughts. She checked the clock. The night nurse was apparently early. Kara composed herself and went to the door.

When she opened it, Dee was not there. Instead, there was a Hispanic man, likely in his forties. He was the slightest bit overweight, but otherwise rather handsome. Kara thought he looked familiar.

"Hi. I'm Raul," he said in a fully American accent. "I'm Ramon's nephew," he added, spotting the inquiring look on Kara's face.

That explained the familiarity. He was the younger relative Kara had seen in Ramon's pictures.

"Oh. Yes. Of course. Come in."

"Do you know, is my Uncle asleep or—"

"He is still up. He is taking a bath. I am supposed to go get him in ten minutes."

"Wonderful. And you are Mrs—?"

"Gomez. Miss Gomez. Kara Gomez."

She extended her hand and they shook hello.

"A pleasure, Miss Gomez. I thought I'd stop by. I feel bad. I was supposed to take my uncle to see this guy talk today and I totally got swamped at work and couldn't get free. I felt bad. I know he really wanted to go."

"Oh, but we did go," said Kara. "I took him."

"You took him?" said Raul surprised.

"Paul drove us. But I watched the talk with him."

"Thanks so much Miss Gomez. That was really nice of you. That's above and beyond the job description."

"I did not mind," said Kara, thinking of Dan. She quickly noticed that the thought of Dan didn't hold quite the same impact now that she was here, talking to Raul.

"Well I really appreciate it. Listen if you want to head home, feel free. I'll keep Ramon company until the night nurse arrives."

"Oh. I don't know. They do pay me to be here."

"I won't tell. I'll make sure Ramon doesn't either."

"Oh. Okay then. You are very kind."

"I suppose I am, aren't I?" Raul said with a mildly flirtatious smile.


On her bus ride home, Kara thought about Raul. Meeting him hadn't sent her heart racing in the way that meeting Dan had, but he did seem charming and he was attractive, if a bit old for her.

Of course, he might be married. But she hadn't noticed a wedding ring on his fingers when they shook hands. She also knew it might not be proper to romantically pursue the nephew of her client. But she could have sworn he was flirting towards the end of their interaction.

When she arrived at her apartment, she opened her door and Ricki flew towards her, giddy at the return of her owner. Kara readily accepted her attack of licks, grateful for the physical affection. She had spent too much of the day imagining affection without actually receiving any.

She settled in. She shed her work clothes and put on a comfortable pair of pajamas. She pulled a TV dinner (Beef Bolognese) out of the freezer and zapped it to edible in the microwave.

She pulled up her coffee table, to use as dinner table, and sat on the couch. Ricki immediately took this as a cue to curl up beside her. She used Kara's thigh as a pillow.

She put on the TV and watched an episode of "Apuseta por un Amor", a telenovela, on Univision. The show, as was typical, was filled wall to wall with passionate kisses and declarations of love. Even though she was fully aware of the program's lack of realism, watching it made Kara desire someone to have by her side all the more intensely. (There were also cheesy murders and over the top declarations of hate on the show, but Kara mostly ignored those since they didn't apply to her mindset). She finished her meal and lay down with Ricki, comforted by her giddy panting and warm fur, jealously watching beautiful actresses get kissed by handsome actors.

Now that it had been over two hours and her phone call had not been returned, she became certain that the Dan ship had sailed. She refocused her beacon of romantic hope on Raul. She would have to learn more about him. She could try to subtly question Ramon, so that he would only think she was making conversation.

She was mulling over her strategy for inquiring about Raul when her phone rang. She jumped, startling Ricki and sending her into a fit of barking.

"Shush!" she said, anxiously.

She picked up the phone. It was Dan's number. Her heart rate went rapid. She forced herself to answer.

"Hola," she said, so nervous that she forgot to speak English.


Later in the evening, after dinner ended and Dan said goodbye to Jim, as he was out a bar with Greg and Coady who wanted to celebrate, Dan finally remembered to check his voice mail.

He stepped outside of the bar to inhabit a space quiet enough to hear, and initiated the playback on his phone.

He listened to Kara's message and smiled.

He chuckled at her use of the phrase "money wisdom," in her efforts to pretend she was calling him for reasons of business.

A minute long interaction and a thirty second voice mail certainly weren't enough to get a full impression of a person, but he really liked the partial impression of Kara he currently had. Her message excited him. She seemed to have a sweet intensity which was rather endearing.

Dan considered playing the usual game and waiting to call her back so as to not seem overeager (after all, she had only called two hours earlier), but he also figured that she wasn't playing the game herself (she waited, what, an hour after their meeting to call him?). He selected her number on his phone and hit the dial button.

"Hola," she said, when she picked up after several rings.

"Hola," Dan replied, with an amusing tone.

"Oh. Sorry," she said. "I meant hello."

"I think 'Hola' means the same the same thing as hello," he said. "If I remember from my high school Spanish."

"Yes, I think it does mean the same," she said, laughing.

"I'm glad we cleared that up."

"Yes, me too."

"This is Dan McCoy by the way," he said.

"Yes, I know."

"Just making sure. I didn't want you to think I was just some random creep calling to give you Spanish lessons."

"No, no, I did not," she said, laughing again.

"Good. And this is Kara then?"

"Yes, I am Kara."

"I'm returning your message Kara. This is the official message return call."

"Thank you for returning my message," she said, somewhat flirtatiously.

"You are quite welcome," he responded, matching her tone. "I understand you are looking to gain some of my money wisdom."

"Yes, I would love to learn more about...the money wisdom." On her end, she slapped herself, angry that she once again could not come up with a better phrase.

"Well you've come to the right man. Because I have tons of money wisdom.

There is one problem though."

"Oh," she said, discouraged. "What?"

"I can't really give money wisdom over the phone. It would take too long. I would need to meet you in person. Would that be okay?"

"Yes, of course!" she said, too excited to play the game of subtext with him.

"I'm glad to hear it. I'm still in LA for a couple of days so how does dinner tomorrow sound?"

"I can get dinner tomorrow."

"Great. Eight o'clock alright?"

"Eight o'clock is great."

After Kara gave him her address so he could pick her up, they said good-bye and hung up. For a minute afterwards, she remained standing, tense, nerve wracked.

She then processed what had just happened and she leaped into the air. She yelped with joy, scaring Ricki, who fled from the room.

"Sorry Ricki!" she said with laughter. "Come back! Everything is okay. I have a date for tomorrow!"

She collapsed onto her couch and giggled like a school girl. For a split second she thought of calling Teresa before she remembered the horrible truth that she wasn't around anymore to call. Of course, she could never forget that her best friend was dead. It was just so rare for her to feel this kind of excitement about a boy that it instinctively made her think of her childhood and her friend.

Remembering Teresa's death, as always, made her sad. Yet the sadness didn't blot out her happiness. She was sure that Teresa would have wanted her to enjoy her moment of excitement. The last thing Teresa would have wanted is to detract from Kara's joy because of something that had happened to her.

Kara silently thanked her friend for her beyond the grave generosity.

Then she promptly started to worry about what she would wear on her date.

# 4

Kara wore a red dress. She hadn't worn it for over two years. The last time the dress saw the outside of a closet was a long ago evening in a Tijuana club with Teresa. In fact, Kara's whole wardrobe of "night out" outfits had done nothing but gather dust since Teresa died. On her online dates Kara had worn far more subdued dresses, fit for Sunday mornings at church.

She wanted to impress Dan. Especially since she had been wearing scrubs the first time they met. She squeezed into the tight outfit. She was worried momentarily that it no longer fit but she forced it on and the couple of pounds she had gained accentuated her curves in it perfectly. She topped her makeup off with bright red lip stick.

When she came to the door, Dan was blown away. She looked absolutely stunning. He had already been quite attracted to her when she was dressed in sanitary cotton and polyester teal. This was another level entirely. He had to rein himself in to make sure he didn't drool like a cartoon wolf.

"Hi," he said.

"Hi," she replied.

Dan wore his usual blazer and dress shirt with no tie. Kara worried that she had over-dressed. Would he think she was over eager? Would he be turned off by her taking a first date far too seriously?

"It is nice to see you again," said Dan.

"You as well," said Kara.

She looked so good, Dan almost felt impure giving her a compliment; like a little boy sinfully sneaking a peak at a female body when he's not supposed to be looking. He reminded himself that he was a grown adult on a date.

"You look beautiful," he said.

"Thank you." She looked embarrassed.

Kara had an air about her that Dan found incredibly appealing. A mixture of sensuality and innocence. Fire and purity. She looked beautiful in the way of a woman who was unaware of the extent of her beauty. He liked that.

As Dan opened the door to his Mercedes and let her take the passenger seat, Kara worried that he would sense her overwhelming nervousness. She took a deep breath as he walked over to the driver's side to let himself in. She made a split second prayer for some composure. She prayed that Dan would be everything she hoped.

Dan settled himself in his seat and started the ignition with a push of a button. Kara's eyes widened with amazement. He smiled.

"Have you never seen that before?"

"No."

"These new cars, you don't put a key in anymore. You keep it in your pocket and it wirelessly alerts the cars you're there and then you push this button. It's a safety procedure. Makes them harder to steal."

"Oh."

"Also, it's cool. I'm pretty sure they do it this way about fifty percent for coolness. Maybe more."

Kara laughed. "It is cool."

"Absolutely it is."

He took her to a restaurant called Perrot. It was a fancy establishment, complete with dim lighting and crisp white table cloths. Kara was intimidated. She didn't often feel self-conscious about her race living in Los Angeles, but walking into Perrot, the fact that she was Mexican suddenly felt very pronounced. Los Angeles had a very large population of Hispanics and she had rarely been the only member of her race anywhere she had ventured. This was not the case at Perrot.

Kara didn't see any of the already seated (and all white) patrons turn away from their meals to ogle her with confusion. Still, she suspected that they noticed her and wondered what she was doing in a place like this. She felt second class even though, on the surface, he presence elicited no reaction whatsoever.

Dan noticed the uncomfortable expression on her face.

"Is anything wrong?" he asked, after the hostess seated them.

"No," she said. "It is such a nice place," she said.

He noticed the slight quiver in her voice, but decided not to pursue it.

They dove into the obligatory get-to-know-you small talk while they looked over their menus.

Kara asked about his work. He briefly explained the nature of his profession. Dan asked her if she was from Los Angeles and she explained that she was from Tijuana and was in the U.S. on a student Visa. He asked about her studies. She asked him if he was born in Los Angeles and he explained that he didn't even live in Los Angeles. He lived in San Diego. He spotted the concerned look on her face and assured her that it was only a little over two hours by train. Kara wasn't particularly pleased to hear that he lived in a different city, but she was so excited to be on a date with such an impressive man that she didn't let it discourage her.

They ordered their meals. Dan ordered the rosemary braised lamb. Kara ordered the pan-roasted chicken with asiago polenta. Dan got them a pricey bottle of wine.

"How is your patient?" Dan asked, after the waitress walked away.

"Patient?" she said, distracted by an old man two tables down who she thought she caught looking at her.

"The one you brought to my talk?"

"Oh! He is good!" she said, feeling stupid. "He mostly slept today."

"That must make your job easier."

She laughed. "That is true. It is easier when he is asleep."

"I guess he's a handful then."

"A handful?" She did not know the expression.

"A headache. A pain. A lot of work."

"Oh. He is not a pain. He's just… He is very dirty."

"Ah. Well I guess that comes with the job, right? They say in life we go in a circle. We start helpless in diapers and that's how we end. If we're lucky. It's a sad state of affairs sometimes. Life."

"What? No, he's not dirty as in not clean. I don't have to clean his… No. I mean he always talks about how pretty I am and he wants to kiss my cheek."

"Oh!" said Dan, laughing. "You mean he's a *dirty old man*. He hits on you."

"Yes! That is it. That is what I mean. He says some things that make me uncomfortable. But I cannot be too mad at him. I do not think he has anyone. He is in this big house all alone. No wife. No children." She thought about Raul, his nephew, but for some reason, decided not to bring him up.

"So he's all by himself. But do you think he's happy that way?"

"Uh… I don't know."

Dan considered making a joke about how he would probably hit on her too if he was an old man, but he decided against it.

He also thought about defending the old man's solitude – explaining to her that he might have decided to be alone by choice and could be very satisfied in doing so. He refrained. He was, he realized, just feeling unnecessarily defensive against the usual comments disparaging his own life philosophy. The last thing he wanted was want to be confrontational with Kara twenty minutes into their date because of statements that other people had made in the past about him. Statements with which Kara might not even agree.

Instead, he asked her about Tijuana.

When the meals arrived Dan saw that Kara looked confused.

"What?" he asked.

"Did you order appetizers?"

"No. Did you want some?" he said. Then he looked down at his meal and realized what she was asking.

Their orders were presented with terrific artistry. They looked delicious. They were, however, extraordinarily small.

Dan felt like her had let her down. Never a feeling one wants to have on a first date.

"These are what we ordered," he said glumly.

Kara looked shocked.

"This? That's all!" she said, completely unable to comprehend. It was rather charming.

Dan decided that the best way to save face would be to play along with her indignation.

He took three quick big bites of the lamb on his plate and finished the dish in its entirety.

"Well I'm stuffed," he said sarcastically.

Kara laughed. "No, no, no, no, no. This is no good. No good at all." She brightened up. "I have an idea."

"What's that?" said Dan. He leaned in, delighted to hear what she had to say.


She took him to the boardwalk at Venice Beach.

There was a taqueria she had spotted on several occasions. Kara had never eaten there but something about the design of the place reminded her of home. She had wanted to try it for a while but she rarely ate outside of her apartment. It was less expensive that way and besides, she usually had no one to eat with.

Her excitement grew as she and Dan approached the window.

"Oh. You are going to love this. I just know. This will be delicious!" she said.

Dan thought her enthusiasm was very attractive.

"I don't know," he said, playing the game of contradictory flirtation. "I just don't know if your opinion can be trusted."

She was too focused on the food to take his bait and pretend to be offended. "You will love it," she assured, with confidence.

They approached the window and Kara took over the proceedings. She was all business.

"We would like two al pastor, two carne asada, two chorizo suadero y carnitas, and two mahi-mahi," she said.

She turned to Dan. He stared at her, wide eyed.

"Oh," she said, suddenly self-conscious. "Do you mind that I ordered for you?"

"Not at all," Dan said convincingly. "I like a woman who takes charge."

"Twenty-two dollars," said the taqueria employee.

Kara reached for her wallet, but Dan grabbed her hand.

"Wait a moment. I don't like a woman who takes charge *that* much."

"You paid for the other dinner," she said.

"That was our appetizer, this is our main course. I insist."

"Okay then," said Kara, who was less focused on the discussion of who would pay for the tacos and more focused on Dan's hand, which lingered on her own. She wanted it to stay there all night but she was all worried that he felt her whole body shaking. It had been a while since a man had touched her.

When the tray was brought to them, it was nearly overflowing with tacos.

"Well we certainly won't go hungry here," said Dan.

"Perhaps I ordered too much," said Kara.

"Nonsense."

They sat down at an outside table.

"These smell amazing," said Dan.

"Eat! Eat!" Kara insisted.

They dug in. Dan's eyes rolled back into his head in ecstasy.

"Oh my god," he said. "These are *delicious*."

Kara was less enthusiastic. "They are…okay," she said.

"*Okay?* I think these are the best tacos I've ever had."

"More than okay. They are good," she admitted. She thought of how to explain her reaction. "But…there is something missing."

Dan peeked into his taco. "Did they forget something?" he said. "I'll go tell them to make us new ones."

"No, no," she said, smiling at his misinterpretation. "What I mean is… there is no *love* in these tacos."

Dan said nothing for a moment. He tried to gauge whether she was making a joke. When he realized she was serious, he said, "No love? What…?"

"I mean, there is no sense of history. No sense of place. Of time. Yes they are good, but…these are California tacos. *American* tacos. They are not the same as Mexican tacos."

Dan's expression became very serious. Kara wondered if she had offended him. He picked up his taco and looked at it very closely.

Then he said, with the utmost earnestness, "You're right. There's not a shred of love in these tacos."

He slammed the taco onto his tray and looked around in mock outrage. "Sir, I demand a refund! There is no love in these tacos! I will not – nay, I *cannot* eat these tacos! Take them away!"

Kara burst out laughing. She picked up a taco and bit into it. "Do not get me wrong," she said. "They are good."

Dan looked right into her eyes. Her eye direction flickered away momentarily, emotionally intimidated, but she wanted to look at him badly and she made herself look back.

"If you're happy," he said. "I'm happy."

When they finished their second, more filling meal, they walked the boardwalk for a while.

"Do you have a large family?" Dan asked, as they strolled.

Kara thought of the last time she had been asked that question, by bread-stick loving Tony. She laughed.

"What's funny?" said Dan.

"Nothing. I just thought of another date I was on recently."

"Oh?" said Dan, feeling oddly threatened.

"The man was nice, but he was not very appealing. He asked me about my family and when I tried to answer he would not listen because he was too busy in his trying to get more breadsticks from the waitress."

Dan laughed. "Well I promise I'll listen to your answer. Luckily there are no breadsticks around to distract me."

"Yes, lucky," she said.

Kara told him all about the various factions of her large clan. When she finished, she asked Dan about his own family.

He hesitated. He had no desire to speak about his family. He felt stupid having asked her about her family and not having expected the socially obvious reciprocal question.

"Small family," he said.

"Do you have brothers or sisters?" she asked.

"Yeah, I have an older sister, but I don't see her that much" he said warmly enough, though he wanted to change the subject.

He turned to the ocean. "Wow, look at those waves Kara."

"They are very nice?" she said, confused.

"Those are some really good surfing waves. I tell you what. If I wasn't having such a good time with you, I would probably run out there right now and see what I could do."

She smiled at the not so subtle compliment. "You don't have a surf board," she said.

"That's true. But if I wanted to surf bad enough, I'd chop down one of these trees and build one."

"Or you could buy one at one of these stores. Like that one, or that one, or that one," she said playfully, pointing out the many stores on the boardwalk which did in fact, sell surf boards.

"Okay, okay, I get your point." He laughed.

"How long have you surfed?"

"Since I was a kid. About fifteen. Have you ever tried?"

"No."

"Oh, Kara. It really is one of the best feelings in the world when you catch a wave correctly. There are few things more thrilling."

"What about sky jumping?"

"You mean sky diving?"

"The jump out of a plane"

"Yeah, sky diving. Sky diving is pretty thrilling."

"Sometimes I think I would like to try that. Other times I think I would die before I jump out of a plane."

Dan laughed and looked at Kara for a long moment. He wanted to look longer but he forced his eyes away. He felt an intense affection growing for her by the moment, such as he hadn't felt for a new woman in a very long time. Plus, it didn't hurt that she was outrageously sexy.

Kara noticed Dan looking at her and she felt a huge surge of joy careen back and forth from her head to her toes. The date had been everything she hoped it would be. *Could it be*, she wondered, *did I finally find what I'm looking for?* She knew that she should temper her expectations somewhat. It had only been one date. But she couldn't help herself.

They strolled the beach walk for a while longer. Dan talked more about surfing. Kara talked more about the food back in Mexico. They mutually delighted each other with everything they had to say.

At some point Dan checked his watch and realized it was getting late.

"I guess I should probably take you home," he said, a hint of disappointment in his voice.

"Yes, it is getting late" she said, equally bittersweet.

When they arrived at Kara's apartment building Dan got out of the car and walked around to help Kara from the passenger seat.

"Thanks," she said, thinking his assistance was a little silly, but feeling intensely grateful for it anyway.

"May I walk you to your door?" he asked.

"Yes please," she said.

Kara extended her arm and he wrapped his own arm around it. They walked the short walk to the door.

"Well here we are," he said.

"Yes, we have arrived."

There was a moment of silence.

Dan broke it. "Kara, I have to admit, I'm a little confused," he said, suddenly serious.

"Why?" she asked, concerned.

"Well I returned your call, and we've spent all this time together tonight… and you haven't once asked me for financial advice. I'm beginning to think that wasn't really why you wanted to see me at all."

She cracked up laughing.

"You are a smart man, Daniel McCoy," she said. "I cannot fool you."

"I knew it! You're very sneaky Kara. I have to watch out for you."

"I guess so."

"I had a really wonderful time tonight Kara," he said, dropping the jokes and deciding it was time to be genuine.

"Yes, so did I."

"I'd like to see you again. Do you think you'd like to see me again?"

"Yes. I would like that very much."

They both went quiet. Dan, uncharacteristically nervous, contemplated just how to attempt the kiss he desperately wanted to plant on Kara's lips. He didn't have to think for long, because Kara beat him to it. Wanting to show him how much she liked him, she thrust herself forward and kissed him passionately.

When they finally pulled apart, all Dan could manage to say was "Wow."

Kara didn't say anything. She just smiled. Her smile was a strange mixture – half embarrassed at her own aggression, half devilish, indicating there was plenty more where that came from.

"So," said Dan, composing himself. "I head back to San Diego tomorrow. But if you want, you could come down next weekend? I don't have much planned except for a couple of client phone calls, so we could spend some time together." Dan usually might have been hesitant to invite a woman to spend a weekend at his place after one date (more because of her possible discomfort than anything else), but Kara's kiss made him figure he didn't need to play it so safe.

"That sounds great," she said, feeling fully prepared to say yes to any request Dan made of her, no matter how intrusive or insane. "I will come down and see you in San Diego."

"Really? You will?"

"Yes. I would love that."

"Terrific. So I'll call you later this week and set it up?"

"Yes. That works."

"Great. Well goodnight Kara."

They kissed again. This time Dan took it upon himself to initiate.

Kara pulled away slowly. Dan probably would have kissed her all night.

"Goodnight Daniel," she said.

She walked into her front door. She looked over her shoulder and smiled as she disappeared inside, performing her best impression of a seductress.

It worked. Dan was left alone on the doorstep, consumed with desire.

Kara maintained her composure until she entered her apartment and closed the door. Then she fell backwards against the wall and let out a yelp of pure joy.

Ricki came bolting from the pile of blankets where she was resting and jumped onto her.

Kara picked her up and spun her around with delight.

"Oh, Ricki," she said, feeling blissful.

# PART II:
## JUNE – AUGUST 2013

# 5

"Here are your pills Ramon," said Kara, chipper as a bird on the first day of spring.

"You know Kara, I've been taking the pills you give me every day and you still haven't agreed to even one little kiss," he said, expecting to get a rise out of her.

Kara paused for a moment, then leaned in and kissed him on the cheek. Ramon nearly fell out of his bed. His jaw hung open. He wanted to speak but no sound came out. Kara laughed.

"What's gotten into you?" he finally said.

"Nothing," she said, unable to hold in her glee.

"Is it a man?" he asked.

"Maybe," said Kara, like an eleven year old girl hiding her first crush.

Ramon took over Kara's usual job and rolled his own eyes.

"Of course."

"Oh Ramon," she said. "Are you jealous?"

Her good mood inspired her to show off her spunk on the job in a way she normally wouldn't.

"You should have seen the women I was with in my younger days," he said, regaining his composure.

"I am sure they were beautiful," she said.

"And plentiful," he added.

"Good for you Ramon," she said. Then she immediately left the room, leaving the old man staring.

Kara went to the kitchen to clean up and make Ramon's lunch. She was absolutely giddy. It was Friday afternoon. The next day she would be on a train to see Dan in San Diego.

They had only talked once during the week. On Wednesday night he had called her to confirm the specifics of the plans. The phone call was brief but it was charged with excitement.

"I'm really looking forward to seeing you again," he had said and Kara could tell that he meant it.

She had maintained her composure at work throughout the week, but, she supposed, now that the weekend peeked its wonderful head around the corner, she could no longer restrain her happiness.

Dan sprayed two bursts of 409 onto the counter top and wiped away any remaining hidden grime with a paper towel. He thought he had spotted a lingering smudge, although how it could have survived his fire bomb of cleaning, it was impossible to say.

Dan liked his place clean – it would be an understatement to say. He had a chronic, gut-level hatred of dirt might be more accurate.

He had a cleaning woman come every two weeks and she did a good job, but he found that still wasn't enough to satisfy his germ extermination protocol. Dan's usual policy was to clean up any dirt or mess or grime or dust the first moment he spotted it. He was aware that he liked his place more spotless than most people would, but he couldn't really comprehend why everyone's cleaning policy wasn't the same as his. *If you see the dirt, clean it up. It's the easiest way to keep things clean. Why look at a piece of dirt and ignore it?* It really did baffle him.

With Kara coming this weekend, his desire for spotlessness was amped up to new levels. He wasn't even certain that she would come back to his place, though he had his hopes, and he wanted to be sure if things did go in that direction the house would be one hundred percent grime free for her visit.

Dan was fairly amped to see Kara. If he didn't know himself so well, he might have even thought he was nervous. But that was impossible. Dan hadn't been made nervous by a female since his first kiss at eleven years old.

He was just excited. That, in and of itself, was still notable.

Contrary to the popular belief of his friends, Dan quite liked being in a relationship. He had never had much interest in one night stands or weekend flings. He found the regular implications that he was a commitment-phobe a little insulting since his romantic history was made up almost entirely of long term relationships. Just because he didn't like to arbitrarily agree to spend the rest of his life with someone, long past the point of any affection on the part of either party, didn't mean that he wasn't completely committed to someone when he was with them.

After the eight years with Rebecca he had been in another relationship which lasted a year and a half. Before Rebecca he had been in relationships which lasted three years, two years, one year, and three and a half years, respectively.

Even when he had been in high school and college Dan never had any interest in just adding sexual conquest notches to his belt. Unlike many of his friends, he had never cheated on a girlfriend, because he believed that if he desired someone else more than the woman he was with, it was time for that relationship to end.

Still, he couldn't remember the last time he had felt so excited by someone so quickly after meeting them. His memory might have to go all the way back to his first serious relationship, in high school.

He sat down. Never one to spend his time reliving lost moments, Dan hadn't thought about Jennifer in a long time. She was his first love. The first girl he ever slept with. And his first experience of love's fickle nature. When they started to argue with alarming regularity at the end of senior year after being together for over two years, Dan felt panicked and baffled. He had expected what they had to go on and on and he held on to it for far longer than he should have. It took a full year of increasingly harsh division before they considering calling it quits as an option.

Once out of the fire, Dan was able to look at the situation more practically. *Where is it written that love is forever?* he asked. *Nowhere*, he determined. From then on he accepted the temporary nature of relationships from the get go. He felt certain that all relationships were inherently impermanent, regardless of whether people overruled their emotions and stayed in them.

He had loved many women since Jennifer but he had never felt the overcoming magnetic pull of desire to the same extent since. The beginning was always too informed by the inevitable ending.

He felt that pull again now.

Over the years Dan had proven himself right time and time again when every love he shared eventually faded way. Every piece of real world evidence confirmed his theory.

Whatever he felt for Kara right now he would not let himself forget the truth of where these things always ended.

Of course, that didn't mean he couldn't have a great time with her this weekend.

Kara peered out the window as her train pulled into San Diego's Santa Fe Depot train station. Next to her, in her pet carrier, Ricki made a couple of yips and the woman sitting across the aisle from Kara gave her another dirty look. She had been giving Kara dirty looks the entire train ride – every time Ricki made even the smallest peep.

Kara wanted to yell at the woman; to tell her that she didn't intend to bring her dog on a second date but that she couldn't think of a single person to ask to watch her. *What was I supposed to do with her!* She wanted to scream in the annoyed lady's face.

Instead she turned her eyes back towards the window. A moment later, all her frustration dissipated when she spotted Dan waiting for her on the platform. She forgot about the woman completely and her stomach twisted itself in knots.

As the train screeched to a halt, Kara reached overhead and grabbed the small overnight bag she had brought with. Before leaving she had argued with herself for an hour as to whether to pack as if she intended to stay over. Dan had not expressly invited her to stay. He had only asked her to come down "for the evening." Then again, it was over a two hour train ride. *He couldn't really expect her to return to LA that night, could he?*

She didn't want to presume that he wanted her to stay, but if he did, she didn't want to come unprepared. It was a real dilemma because whatever her packing choice, her bag, or lack of bag, would declare her intentions right away.

She gathered up Ricki and her bag and proceeded off the train.

Dan spotted her walking down the platform and waved. They approached each other, meeting in the middle.

He was so pleased to see her that he didn't even notice the canine in her left hand until Ricki barked.

Dan's primary reaction to Ricki's presence was more confusion than anything else. *Why would she have brought a dog?*, he thought. Then, after the initial shock, displeasure took over. He was no big fan of pets. It amazed Dan how people held themselves to a certain standard of cleanliness, but then would allow filthy animals who sniffed and licked poop to lick their faces and traipse around their homes.

Kara spotted the look on Dan's face and rushed to explain. The last thing she wanted was to start out the day on a sour note.

"Please forgive me for having to bring Ricki," she said. "My friend was going to watch her but she canceled at the last minute," she made up.

"That's okay, don't worry about it," Dan forced himself to say, unconvincingly. "Here, let me help you."

He took Ricki's cage. The pooch barked at him aggressively but he did his best to ignore it.

"I got us a dinner reservation at a great place. And don't worry – I double checked that the meals are normal sized."

Kara laughed. "Good," she said.

"So I originally thought we would go straight there, but I can call to push back the reservation and we can drop off the dog—"

"Ricki. Her name is Ricki. I guess I did not introduce you! Sorry. Dan, this is Ricki. Ricki, this is Dan."

Ricki growled.

"A pleasure Ricki," Dan said with obviously feigned enthusiasm. "We can drop of Ricki at my place and then we can go to the restaurant," he said.

"Is your place out of the way?"

"Yeah, a little, but it's not big deal. I don't mind."

Kara said nothing for a moment. She didn't like the idea of leaving Ricki all alone for hours at a house she wasn't familiar with.

"Let's just bring her with us," she suggested lightly. "Then we don't have to call the restaurant."

"I don't…bring her with us?"

"Yeah! Then she doesn't have to be lonely."

"Well, she can't come in the restaurant."

"She will wait in the car."

"She'll be just as alone in the car as at my place."

"Not for as long."

"She'll have to be in her cage."

"Why will she have to be in her cage?"

"You want her to just be out, in the car?"

"Of course!"

"I…" Dan paused. He did not want to the ruin this second date with a woman he was so excited to see by getting into a bizarre argument right off the bat. "So you want Ricki to come with us tonight?"

"She must!" said Kara, happily. Having grown up in a family of dog lovers Kara could not register the idea that someone would be turned off by an adorable pooch. She did not grasp how hard it was for Dan to give in on the subject.

After a long pause Dan said, "If she must, she must!" He hoisted Ricki's cage up to his face. "C'mon Ricki, let's go!"

When they got to the parking lot, Kara let Ricki out of her cage so she could pee, following the long train ride.

She stood still on her four legs and stared up at Dan and Kara.

"I don't think she's going to go," said Dan after a long, quiet minute.

"Maybe not," said Kara. "She does not like the concrete. We will have to find her some grass."

On the way to the restaurant they stopped again. This time at a patch of grass. Ricki was just as resistant.

"Hmmm," said Kara. "I guess she just does not have to go."

Any mild tension over Ricki vanished completely at dinner. With the pup safely locked in Dan's Mercedes (*slobbering all over the seats, I'm sure,* Dan thought with an internal shrug of the shoulders), they were able to resume their delighted flirtation right where it left off the weekend before.

"I'm glad you came down," Dan said.

"I am too."

"I was worried some other guy might sweep you up into his own whirlwind of romance before I had a chance to see you again."

"There were a few men on the train," she said facetiously. "But I did not think I could use them for money advice, so I turned them down."

Dan laughed. "Oh right. I forgot you were just using me for money advice."

"You forget so quick."

"Well I guess we should get started talking about stocks then."

"No. There is time for that later."

"You're planning on using me for a while, huh?" he said, full of innuendo.

Kara blushed. "Maybe," she said.

Just as Dan promised, the meals, when they came, were normal sized.

"Any love in your salmon?" Dan asked seriously after Kara had begun to eat.

"A touch," she said. "Could maybe use another dab but I think it is good."

"Good, I'm glad," said Dan.

After dinner, they let Ricki out to pee again, but the dog continued to have no interest in emptying her bladder.

Kara shrugged her shoulders. "I don't understand it," she said. "Maybe she's just nervous."

Dan was in a good mood after dinner and was no longer so concerned about Ricki.

"Oh well," he said. "She'll go when she goes. So listen. I've got an idea for where to go next that I think you're going to love."


As soon as they walked in to El Club Tigre, Dan began to think his bright idea of where to take Kara was not actually so bright.

In the week between their date, Dan had asked around as to where to find the most "authentic" Mexican bar in San Diego. He thought taking her to such a place would impress her, after the conversation they had at the taqueria in Los Angeles.

Within seconds of entry though, Dan realized he might be in over his head.

He had expected a bar which also had room for dancing. What he walked into was a vibrant, loud, wall to wall salsa dance club. There was only the smallest sliver of non-dancers along a far wall. Everyone else was moving their bodies with pulsating precision to the music. Dan was well aware that his own dancing ability was less than stellar.

"This is great!" Kara declared upon seeing the spot. "Very Mexican," she said to please Dan, since she knew he wanted to impress her. In actuality the differences between El Club Tigre and a club in Mexico were readily apparent to her, but she was still delighted enough by the place not to be bothered by them.

She turned to Dan noticed an apparent look of sickness on his face.

"Are you okay?" she asked.

It was a moment of truth. Dan could admit, with embarrassment, his painful inability to dance; or he could hope something miraculous would seize hold of his body and grant him heretofore unknown rhythm.

"Just fine," he said after deliberation. "I had something caught in my eye." He pretended to wipe his eye. "There, I got it."

Kara grabbed his hand. "C'mon, let's go," she said, leading him onto the dance floor.

It only took about thirty seconds for Kara to realize Dan suffered from a severe case of double left feet.

At first she tried to help him. She offered nuggets of instruction.

"No you have to more your feet like…"

"No your arm should not be in this position…"

"No if just turn more this way…"

Eventually she just stopped dancing herself and watched his efforts. He was concentrating so hard on his painfully graceless movement that he didn't even notice his partner had stopped dancing.

She felt a burst of laughter coming on and tried to contain it, but she couldn't help herself.

Dan heard her laugh. He looked up and stopped dancing.

"What?" he said, though he knew the answer quite well.

"I am sorry Daniel," she said. "But you are not the best dancer I have seen."

For a moment he was mortified. Then he took a deep breath and felt quite calm. Now that it was out in the open, he might as well be in on the joke.

"Maybe I could use a little work," he said with a laugh.

"Maybe more than a little work, I think," she said.

"You don't like these moves?" he said, breaking back into his jagged, clumsy dance routine.

She laughed. He pulled her in.

"Show me what to do again," he said.

She tried to instruct him once more to no avail.

"No, show me," he said. "Physically force me. Be rough baby, I can take it." He grabbed her hands and put them on his own arms.

She giggled as she swung his arms and legs around like a puppet. A couple of the dancers near them looked over, wondering what the hell was going on.

Kara leaned her head up against his chest, unable to control her laughing fit. "I cannot stop laughing!" she said.

Dan lifted her chin up. "I think I know a cure for that," he said.

He kissed her. That did the trick.


They gave up their attempts at dancing and had drinks against the wall with the thin sliver of non-dancers.

When they left the club and reemerged into the quiet parking lot, the boom of salsa still vibrating in their ear canals, Dan said, "Umm…yeah…so if you never want to see me again after that performance, I understand."

She smiled big. "No, do not worry about it Daniel. I still would like to see you."

Dan looked at his watch. It was nine thirty.

"So the last train to LA leaves at ten fifteen. We have to hurry if you're going to make that."

Dan said it in a way which made it sound optional.

Kara paused. She did not want to go home and felt a surprising lack of shyness in being forward.

"You know, if you do not mind," she said, "Why don't you show me your place?"

Dan smiled. "You might miss your train."

Kara shrugged her shoulders.

"If I miss it, I miss it," she said.

Kara felt empowered, taking such charge. A lifetime of passivity was toppling over and Dan was the necessary spark to light the fuse. She felt really *good* for the first time in a long time. She felt not just the potential for happiness, but actual happiness, right there, burning inside her. She had forgotten just how good it felt.

Kara let Ricki out to pee once more in front of Dan's condo. Once again, she refused to go.

"I don't understand you Ricki," she said. Then Kara lifted the dog up, cradled her in her arms like a baby, and followed Dan inside.

He flipped on the lights.

"Here we are."

Kara looked around. The place was magnificent. Spare, minimalistic, but beautiful. Kara didn't know much about interior design but she knew a well-crafted living space when she saw one. The hardwood floors were perfectly accentuated by the well placed art on the walls and the expensive looking furniture. On the far right side, a balcony overlooked the beach and the ocean.

"It is beautiful Dan," she said.

Kara casually placed Ricki on the floor, thinking nothing of it. Dan eye's locked on the pooch as she sniffed around. His heart beat a little harder. Then he forced himself to look at Kara. *I don't have to be so neurotic about this*, he though. *It's just a dog.*

"Thanks. I'm glad you like it."

Kara's eyes suddenly went very wide.

"What?" said Dan.

He whipped his head in the direction of Kara's eye sight. Ricki was in the middle of peeing on his expensive shag rug.

"Ricki!" yelled Kara. She ran over to her but it was too late. The dog shook herself off and admired her handiwork.

"Bad dog! Bad dog!" said Kara.

Dan was briefly catatonic. He shook his head and snapped himself out of it.

"I am so so sorry," said Kara, mortified.

"You know what?" said Dan. "Don't worry about it."

He walked over to the rug and rolled it up. He hoisted it on his shoulder, walked to the front door, opened the door, and threw the rug onto the front lawn.

"I wanted a new rug anyway," he said.

The tension cut, Kara burst out laughing. "I really am sorry. What a little bitch," she said, scolding Ricki.

Dan laughed with her. "Literally," he said.

"What?"

"Nothing. Can I get you something to drink? Would you like some wine?"

"Do you have any milk?" asked Kara, as if it was a completely normal request.

"Sure," said Dan, with a sideways smile, enjoying every new quirk of this girl that presented itself. "I have some milk."

He went to the kitchen. He poured Kara a glass of milk and poured himself a glass of wine. When he came back, Kara was standing by the balcony, looking out at the ocean

"You don't mind if I have wine?" he said when he handed her the milk.

"By all means necessary!"

Dan chuckled. "I think you were going for, 'by all means.'"

"Oh, sorry," she said, slightly embarrassed. "My English is still not always the best."

"I love the way you talk, actually," said Dan.

He raised his glass.

"To a lovely evening," he said.

"A lovely evening," Kara seconded.

They clinked their glasses and drank.

"Thank you for the milk," said Kara. "I do not normally drink alcohol. The club earlier was unusual for me."

"My pleasure. I'm sure you needed a drink earlier after seeing me dance."

She laughed, then continued to look out at the ocean.

"It's a beautiful view," she said.

"It is," he said, looking at Kara and ignoring the ocean.

He placed his glass down and put his arm around her waist.

Kara put her own glass down and slowly turned towards him. He kissed her slowly.

"Shall I show you the upstairs?" he said, after a minute.

Kara nodded her head. She looked eager and shy, simultaneously.

He took her hand and led the way.

In his room, he took her shoulders and laid her down on his bed while he continued to kiss her. He was both powerful and gentle in a way that turned her on dramatically.

Uncharacteristically forward, unable to contain her desire, she slid her hand down his pants.

He smiled then responded in kind, peeling her dress off her like a sexed up orange peel, kissing each part of her body as it was revealed.

He lowered himself on top of her and she wrapped her free arm around his back.

Their bodies seemed perfectly molded for their particular connection. The pleasure was immense. They stared into each other's eyes and the rest of the world disappeared.

They melted into one another.

# 6

The next morning Kara awoke to the smell of breakfast.

She took her time exiting Dan's exquisite bed. Wrapped up in his silk sheets, she smelled his pillow and basked in the afterglow of the dreamlike evening. The sunlight broke through the eastern window, shining down and warming her up. Eventually she forced herself up. Her overnight bag and her spare clothes were downstairs, so she raided Dan's drawers. She put on a pair of exercise sweat pants and a tee shirt.

Emerging into the kitchen, she found Dan hard at work on a morning meal which could feed five. Eggs, sausage, bacon, toast, potatoes, filled plated and frying pans.

"Good morning," he said, spotting her.

"Good morning," she said. She walked over and kissed him. "Oh my, this is too much," she said, taking a thorough look at the breakfast buffet he was concocting.

"There is no such thing as too much," he said with assurance.

As it turned out, there was. Neither of them made a dent in the pile of food.

"Oh well," Dan chuckled. "I felt like cooking."

"It was delicious," she said.

"I guess I was still concerned about the whole small portions thing from the first restaurant. I didn't want to disappoint you, so I overcompensated."

Ricki, not exactly an early riser, wandered into the kitchen.

"Look who is up!" said Kara, excited.

"Hi Ricki," said Dan, much less enthusiastic.

Ricki jumped onto two legs against Dan, propping herself up with her front paws against Dan's shin. Dan awkwardly attempted to pet Ricki by patting her on the head repeatedly like she was a lid he wanted to force onto a jar.

Kara, not entirely unperceptive, laughed at Dan's admirable attempt at animal affection.

"Did you never have a pet as a child?" she asked.

"My sister had a lizard once. Lasted about two months and then she sold it to one of her friends. That was about the extent of pets in the McCoy household."

"You have a sister?"

"Two sisters. I…had two sisters."

Kara did not notice, nor question him, on the specifics of his word usage and he was glad of this. He did not particularly want to talk about family tragedies and bring down his spectacular mood.

Instead she asked, "What was the lizard's name?"

It was such a delightful, unexpected, question that Dan leaned over and gave Kara a long kiss.

When he pulled apart – which Kara was in no rush for him to do – he said with a laugh, "I think its name was Rio actually. Afer the Duran Duran song. She was really into them."

"Duran Duran?"

"You don't know them? I guess that's not a surprise. They don't seem like a band that would have crossed over internationally. They were big in America in the 80s."

"Oh."

"Before your time of course. But they were the years of my youth," he said with a sarcastic wistfulness.

A question suddenly occurred to Kara (who herself was born in 1988) which had not occurred to her before.

"How old are you?" she asked Dan.

He paused. He wasn't sure if he heard accusation, or merely curiosity, in her tone.

"I'm not sure I want to tell you," he said, playfully.

"Pleeease," she said, smiling wide, brushing his arm with hand.

He couldn't resist her sudden seduction.

"Fine. I was born in '72."

"I am student of English. Not math," she said.

"Math is the universal language."

"Fine," she said with pretend anger. "I will do the math."

Dan smiled as he watched the gears turn in her head.

"Forty-one!" she said.

"Forty-one," he confirmed.

"You do not look forty one."

"Why thank you my dear."

"No really though. You are so young looking. You have all that hair…"

"Not everyone over forty is bald, Kara."

"That is not what I meant. Your hair is very young."

"It's as old as the rest of me. That's usually how it works."

"Stop it," she said, slapping his arm. Then she paused and thought for a moment. She instinctively looked at his fingers, which were bare. "And you are not married?" she said, somewhat hesitantly. This was another question it had not occurred to her to ask.

"Absolutely not," he said, reassuringly.

"Were you ever married?"

"Never married."

"How come?"

"Not everybody gets married."

"Yes, but you are a handsome, successful man."

"Thanks. I think you're rather attractive yourself."

"I mean, some woman must have wanted to marry you. Forty-one is a long time."

"Hey! It's not that long. You'll be here soon enough."

"But I will be married," she said.

Dan paused. "Will you?" was all he could think to say.

"Of course," she said. She felt almost defensive, though she was not sure why.

The conversation went silent for a moment. Ricki yipped, to express her discomfort with the sudden halt in speech.

Dan didn't particularly want to have this talk right now, on what was still only their second official date. But he also really liked Kara and he didn't want to mislead her.

"Look, Kara," he said, "I should be upfront. I'm not really interested in marriage. Or kids. Those things are great for a lot of people and I understand that. They're just not for me."

Kara took in this information. Or rather, she tried to. Conflicting reactions swirled through her head. On the one hand, the whole reason she wanted to date in the first place was to find a husband so that she could stay in America and continue to support her family. Sure, she wanted a husband and a family anyway, but the visa situation created a pressing need for one right *now*.

On the other hand, last night had been one of the best nights of her life. She *really* liked Dan. He seemed to really like her. The thought of cutting this new relationship off before it had really even begun stung to an almost unbearable degree.

She felt trapped. And as most people do when they find themselves in an unexpected moment of decision for which they are entirely unprepared, twisted up by the uncertainty, she committed to what seemed like the easiest decision at the present moment.

Sitting next to Dan, seeing him look at her with a mixture of affection and sadness, she felt she couldn't possibly stop seeing him. She wanted to spend every moment with him she could, even if he would never marry her.

She put her hand on his.

"I understand," she said, although she didn't. Not really. "We will worry about such things later."

He pulled her in for a long kiss.

*Besides*, she thought. *If he falls in love with me – maybe he will change his mind.*


Dan's discouraging proclamation promptly stored itself in the cluttered, infrequently visited garage of Kara's mind. She couldn't possibly forget what he said, of course. But once she decided to pursue the relationship regardless, she felt that it served no useful purpose to replay a conversation which would only bring down her mood. Kara had felt frustrated and alone for so long and her first couple of dates with Dan were already some of the happiest moments of her life. No, it didn't make any practical sense to date a man who had no interest in a future. But it made emotional sense to keep seeing Dan.

*Things will work themselves out on their own*, she said to herself on the train ride home. *Whatever is meant to be, will be.* Then, she put the subject to rest for the immediate future.

Having banished the only negative moment from the glorious weekend away from her primary thoughts, Kara spent the rest of the week savoring the happiness Dan made her feel. Her effusive mood was so untouchable, she didn't even feel annoyed when at work, Ramon asked her to show him her grapefruits. ("The new ones you just bought with the groceries!" he insisted he meant). Unfortunately for Kara, Ramon mistook her pleasant reaction as evidence that he was making some headway, and thereafter increased his efforts to the ultimate exhaustion of everyone – including him.

Kara and Dan quickly made plans for her to return to San Diego the following weekend. He insisted on paying for her train fee from then on.

Unable to think about any possible future with Dan because of the content of their banished conversation, Kara became extremely present focused. This had an unexpectedly positive effect on her demeanor. She felt very peaceful. When Dan picked her up the following Friday, all thoughts of her visa expiration, her family's financial woes, and her fragile life prospects were nowhere to be found. The only thing on her mind was her delight at seeing this man again after what felt like a month apart, but was only a week.

Dan was equally excited to see her. His feelings were a little more tempered than hers, because of his life experiences which had taught him that passion could disappear without warning at any moment. But he couldn't help but notice his ever growing childlike level of giddiness. He was so happy to see her, he didn't even mind that she had once again brought along Ricki.

As far as the dog was concerned, Kara, uncreatively, gave the same lie – that her friend who was supposed to watch Ricki canceled at the last minute. Dan shrugged it off and accepted that the dog was a permanent part of their relationship. He gave Ricki a cursory, though not entirely unaffectionate, pat on the head. The pooch was a part of the girl. And if he liked the girl so much, he couldn't help but feel some goodwill towards to the pooch.

That second weekend Dan took her to the beach. Kara was surprised when, preparing to depart, he told her to get into a beat up old pick-up truck parked on the side of his condo, rather than the Mercedes he stored in the garage. She questioned him about it. He replied that when he didn't have to project a certain image for his profession he liked to keep himself grounded. To remember his roots. She was quite pleased by this. Kara by no means minded that Dan had money. Still, humility and down-to-earth perception were very appealing in a man as well. She was aware of how rare it was to find a man who had both. She felt lucky.

The weather at the beach could not have been more perfect, nor could the day have felt more perfect. She lay on Dan's chest on a blanket in the sand. She ran around with Ricki, who was both terrified by and intensely curious of the waves. She cajoled Dan into crashing into the water with her and her pet. He held her tight and they kissed as a wave broke. Ricki, shocked, ran from her hands towards the beach. Dan sprinted after the dog and grabbed her not two feet into her trot. Kara fell against them both and laughed.

Dan looked long at Kara as they walked the beach and told her, "God you are beautiful," feeling so attracted to her that he couldn't possibly hold it in one more second. The whole thing was heavenly – ripped straight from the heartwarming conclusion of a romance film.

And so she returned the next weekend, and the next weekend, and the next. Weeks with Ramon and weekends with Dan became her life and all the while the clock ticked down on her status as a legal visitor to the United States of America.

Dan and Kara ate at fancy restaurants and hole in the wall burger joints and international fusion establishments that combined worldly food genres in ways Kara never could have predicted. They went to the symphony and to the movies and to the theater. Or they stayed in at Dan's place for two straight days, almost never leaving the bedroom.

They weren't entirely in sync on every issue. There were times when the flow of conversation slowed or stopped and it suddenly struck them that they were from two entirely different worlds and, on the surface, they had remarkably little in common. But these moments never threatened their growing love for one another. There was something deeper and unclassifiable between them. A connection that could not be explained through puzzle piece explanations of interest or personality. Perhaps their deep, hard to identify similarity came from the kind of muted fire which burned inside both of them. They were both sharply passionate individuals whose natural flame had been curtailed somewhat by harsh circumstances. They each remained outgoing and enthusiastic at heart, but in their public lives their natural state was often covered by a protective shield. Together, their mutual affection and warmth pierced through their respective shields and a not fully familiar optimism leaked out. Maybe therein lay the greatness of them as a couple: they made each other feel optimistic. It also didn't hurt that they were about as physically in sync as two people could be. They seemed to anticipate each other's wants – shifting intuitively from one pleasure to the next, neither the dominant giver nor receiver. When they came together they truly felt like one.

Meanwhile, as their relationship took off, so did Dan's career. The early reviews of Dan's satellite appearances on the financial network were exceedingly positive. Right away the viewers caught on to his unique brand of bluntness and honesty. They liked how he refused to give answers when there were none, gave unexpected answers where uniform opinions were common, and truly seemed to be concerned about the welfare of the little guy in situations that no one else was.

Kara was extremely excited for him, but she was also so caught up in her legal woes that she couldn't invest in her enthusiasm as much as she would have liked. The days ticked by and it was suddenly it was the end of July and Kara was only a month from having to leave the country. As her deadline approached, the all-consuming glee of her relationship with Dan lessened somewhat and her deportation anxiety rose. The only time she was fully able to shed her outer layer of stress was in the actual moments she and Dan were together. Her efforts were fairly comatose. She half-heartedly looked online for a job with enough pull to keep her in the country, but she knew her skills left her unqualified for any such position. Her family really needed the money she was providing and she was helpless to do anything about it.

The big question mark looming down the road became even more pronounced in Kara's mind after a trip home to Tijuana.

The third week in July Kara received a phone call that her brother Ricardo's baby had been born. Her family was having a party in his honor that coming Saturday. She told Dan she had to go down that weekend to see her family but that she would stop in San Diego on the way back.

Meeting the new baby was a joy. Kara was immensely happy for her brother, even if she suffered from her usual light pangs of jealousy. She was now the only child in her family without a child of her own.

Carmen peppered the beauty of the moment with her usual sarcasm.

"Congratulations, baby brother," she said. "Your child is beautiful."

"Thanks Carmen," said Ricardo.

"He must get his looks from his mother because we know he doesn't get them from you!"

"Carmen!" said Kara protectively, though everyone laughed, including Ricardo.

"What? We all know that I'm the one with the looks in the family," said Carmen.

"Is that so?" said Kara.

"Don't feel bad," said Carmen. "You got the brains. That's almost as good as having the looks."

"What did I get?" asked Ricardo.

"You got the luck," said Carmen. "Because Louisa could do a lot better than you!"

Louisa laughed. "Maybe," she said. "But there's nobody else I would want." She kissed her husband.

Later, when she and Kara had a moment alone together, Carmen seized the opportunity to engage in her usual intrusive questioning.

"So how's the gringo?" she said.

Kara and Carmen had not actually had a single conversation about Dan but Kara had told her mother over the phone that she had been dating an American. She supposed it was now common knowledge amongst her hundred closest relatives.

"I would prefer you didn't call him the gringo," said Kara, seriously.

"Is he not a gringo?"

"He's an American."

"What's the difference?"

Kara glared at her sister.

"Fine, fine," said Carmen, chuckling. "How are things with the American?"

"They are good," said Kara. "I like him a lot." She smiled just thinking about him. Carmen could see the affection shine through.

"And how is the sex?" asked Carmen.

Kara became indignant. "Carmen! What kind of a question is that? It is so improper."

"Oh, let go of yourself. It must be really good. I saw the way you smiled then, just thinking about him."

Kara rolled her eyes. She saw that her sister was not going to take her foot off the gas pedal of questioning until she gave a response. "It is very fun," she said.

"Good," said Carmen. "I'm happy for you little sister. You deserve someone who cares for you."

"Thanks," said Kara, in a noticeably sad tone.

"What?" asked Carmen.

"It's just...I am happy, but my visa is going to expire and I'm going to leave him."

"If he's so great, he should marry you so you can stay."

"Well, we've only been together for two months. Besides, he's not that kind of man. He's not really the family type."

"What do you mean?"

"He says he would never get married. To anyone. It's not for him."

"Ah. So he doesn't want the wedding. Just the honeymoon."

"That is one way of putting it."

"You are way too nice Kara. This isn't his decision. It is yours. You must *make* him marry you."

"How would I do that?"

"You use your female charm! You use what God gave you! You tell him he can say goodbye to your body unless he marries you and keeps you in the country. But you say it when he is already…aroused. Men will do anything you ask when they are in that state."

Kara laughed. Carmen really was something.

"Look. I don't want Daniel to marry me because I forced him to or even just so I can get my green card. I would want him to marry me because *he wants* to marry me."

"Kara, he may be a good man. But if he does not marry you, he is a fool."

Kara smiled and put her arm around her sister.

"Thank you Carmen."

On the way to San Diego Kara felt a pressure so intense she thought she might suffocate. She felt like she was tumbling down through the air, just waiting for the inevitable shattering crunch of the ground to catch up to her body. All she wanted was to see Dan. All she wanted was to lie in his arms and forget all her problems. But she knew their imminent meeting wouldn't be so peaceful. It was time for her to tell him about her situation.

Though she had told Dan on their first date that she was in America on a student visa, she hadn't told him that it was going to expire so soon. She had delayed the conversation long enough. Even though she had no expectation that he would change his mind on the topic of marriage – especially since their relationship was still so young – she realized she needed to tell Dan. What was the point of loving someone if you couldn't tell that person about your worries and troubles?

Dan could see something was on Kara's mind from the moment he picked her up. He gave her the courtesy of letting her bring up her concerns if she wanted to, without plodding or interrogation on his part. *If she wants to share what's bothering her*, he thought, *she will do it on her own*. Dan did not believe in openness in a relationship as an absolute. As far as he was concerned, two people could never become one, no matter how similar their personalities or how deeply they loved each other. They could attempt to share everything about themselves and still, they would remain two separate individuals whose respective personas could never be breached. *People are entitled to their privacy no matter how tied they are to someone else*, thought Dan. He didn't want Kara to pry uncomfortably into his thoughts and he would not pry uncomfortably into hers.

Nevertheless, Kara sat him down to share what was bothering her when they arrived at Dan's condo.

"Remember how I said I am in the country on a student visa," she said.

"Of course."

"Yes. Well. The visa I mentioned is going to expire at the end of August."

"Oh," said Dan. "That's soon."

He realized her had never asked her how long she was legally allowed to stay in the country. It seemed an important point and he was angry with himself for not wondering about it.

"What can you do to extend it?" he asked, when she said nothing else.

"I am afraid, there is nothing I can do. My work will not provide a work visa. They can get other caregivers to fill in for me with no problem. I have looked for other work, but I cannot find it."

There was a long silence between them.

"So you have no choice? You have to leave."

"Yes. I think so." She was starting to cry. "Unless…"

"Unless?"

She said nothing, but she looked deep into his eyes and he could tell what she was thinking.

"Nothing," she finally said.

She had not expressed the word out loud but the sound of "marriage," still rang in his ears.

Tearing up Kara said, "I don't know what to do. My father, he should not be working anymore. He is going to hurt himself. My family needs the money I make. But I am going to have to leave and he is going to have to keep working. I am so worried about them."

"There's got to be something we can do," Dan said with force. "They can't just kick you out like this."

"They do it all the time."

The room went silent, except for Kara's tears. Not sure what to say, Dan moved closer to Kara and put his arm around her. She leaned her head against his shoulder and composed herself. She did not wish to completely break down in Dan's presence. She was afraid doing so would lessen his opinion of her.

Dan felt a number of conflicting emotions pounding inside him. Part of him felt fear and aversion. He wanted to run from any ill-thought, heat of the moment commitment. He wanted to be alone, unaffected by such untenable human responsibility. Yet another part of him felt an uncontainable tenderness and love for this girl in his arms whom he had only known for two months. He didn't want to let her go her so quickly. He was just getting to know and love her.

He needed some time to think.

That week the Financial Network asked Dan to fly to New York City for an in-person on-air appearance. Typically he would have been overjoyed at such an opportunity, but other matters occupied him and syphoned away from his pleasure.

When the cameras rolled on his live interview, he delivered his typical charismatic insightful commentary. He responded to each of the host's questions with wit and acuity. After the segment was over and the broadcast cut to commercial, the various employees in the bustling studio took a break from their tasks to give him a nice round of applause. The show's host, a well-respected and esteemed individual, pulled him over for a handshake and gave him fervent words of encouragement. He told Dan he thought he had a bright future with the network.

Yet, Dan felt only half present during the crucial, potentially career-making, proceedings. He had enough focus to do the job that needed to be done, but there was never a second when he stopped thinking about Kara.

At night, Dan turned down offers from a few of the crew on the program to go out for drinks. He would have liked to join them, but he knew he had expended his full ability to concentrate for the day during his live television appearance.

Instead, he settled into his hotel room, took a Corona from the mini-bar, and gazed out into the beautiful Manhattan skyline. Looking out at the twinkling skyscrapers, he felt like he was in another world from his San Diego condo with its ocean view. The oddest sensation of homesickness descended upon him. Dan never got homesick. He loved San Diego with all his heart – he felt it was paradise with its year round perfect temperatures, terrific beaches, and the fairly universal friendliness amongst its citizens – but usually a return his hometown was merely a nice prize waiting for him at the end of a pleasant getaway, not a magnet pulling him back towards it for the necessity of emotional stability. In truth, Dan disliked feeling any sort of weakness, though he was aware all humans had their moments of fragility.

Dan felt restless and before he had a chance to think about what he was doing, he picked up his cell phone and called Kara. Perhaps fortunately, she didn't answer.

"Hi Lovey," he said after her phone went to voicemail. "No need to call me back. It's nothing urgent. I was just looking out at New York, and I have a really gorgeous view from my hotel room, and I was just…wishing you were here with me to share the view. Anyway, I'll be back in San Diego in a couple days. We'll talk soon. I miss you. Bye."

He hung up the phone and collapsed on his bed; yearning, shaken.

*I'm really falling for this girl*, he thought to himself, amazed.

Shortly after, Dan tried to go to sleep, but his attempt was completely pointless. All he did was toss and turn and think about Kara.

Finally, after about an hour, Dan slammed his hand on the bed, sat up straight, flipped on the light, and forced himself to corral his chaotic thoughts.

Just slowing himself down and forcing himself to deal with his feelings rationally, he immediately felt better.

*Okay*, he thought, *what are the key points here?*

*What is it that I really want?*

As soon as he asked it, Dan realized that what he really wanted was for things to continue just as they currently were. Even with his steadily growing feelings for Kara, he didn't necessarily want to see her more than he presently did. The arrangement was perfect; spending time with her on the weekends, separated during the week. It was this sort of consistent separation which made the time they shared together special. Dan was certain that any larger amount of time spent together would ruin it.

She was going to have to leave the country. That seemed to be a fact.

Dan personally wasn't completely averse to the idea of continuing the relationship with her living in Mexico. But he felt pretty confident that she would feel too embarrassed to keep things going in that circumstance, particularly because she wouldn't be able to come visit him with any regularity in San Diego. Likely, he would eventually get fed up with such an arrangement as well.

The unspoken proposition in the air between them was that she would only be able to stay in the U.S. if he married her.

To Kara's credit, she had not actually brought up this possibility. But it was there. He couldn't deny it.

Dan's burgeoning feelings for Kara didn't change his feelings about marriage in the slightest. He still saw it as, at best, unnecessary, and at worse, a detriment to a relationship. He had no desire for kids. He didn't really have any desire to live with another person.

He just wanted things to keep going the way they were. He didn't want this new, wonderful thing to be cut off so soon.

*How can I keep things the way they are?* Dan thought.

Less selfishly, he also thought, *I really, really like this woman. I would love to do something BIG for her. I would love to help her. To give her a great gift.*

*I just don't know if I'm capable of giving her what she needs right now.*

Dan stared out at the Manhattan skyline once again. His confused thoughts rattled and stung and pierced and boomed and then all of the sudden went completely silent. For a moment, his mental stream was calm, infused only with the perceptual gleam of city lights and the honking traffic far below.

Then, a single thought made itself known.

And just like that, Dan knew what to do.


This time it was Dan who seemed like he had something to say when he picked Kara up at the train station. Kara noticed it immediately and her heart plummeted. *It's over*, she thought with certainty.

Dan was morose and uncommunicative. He said hi and kissed her without his usual passion.

For several minutes on the painfully silent ride to his condo, Kara panicked, trying desperately to cling to the blissful dream she had been living for two months, sure she was about to be gracelessly yanked back into the harsh wakefulness of daily dissatisfaction.

She felt hopeless, unsure what to do. Her tear ducts signaled to her that they were ready to start flowing any time. All she had to do was give the word.

But then – just before she broke down and begged Dan to break it off with her then and there instead of torturously making her wait for the "right moment" – she located an unexpected deep source of strength. She wasn't sure of the reason behind her sudden confidence and she didn't question it too deeply. She accepted what was about to come. All hope of remaining in the U.S. was over.

At Dan's condo, he sat her down, just as she expected he would.

Then he started to speak and she prepared herself for the blow.

"I've been doing a lot of thinking," he said. "Finding out that you're probably going to lose your legal status – it's hard, it changes things. While I was in New York I was barely able to sleep. So many things about this were going through my head. And I finally came to the conclusion that there's really only one course of action which makes sense."

Kara closed her eyes.

"I understand," she said, not blaming him in the least for ending things.

Dan reached out for Kara's hands.

"Kara Gomez. Will you fake marry me?"

As if the message was relayed to her via satellite delay, Kara did not understand Dan's words when he spoke them. Ten seconds later, her ears opened up the protective dams which held his sentence back and let the information flood chaotically through her brain. At which point it became apparent that morose resignation was not actually the proper reaction to Dan's words.

"What?" was all that she managed to say.

"I want to marry you so that you can get your green card. I want to help."

"You want to *fake* marry me?" she said, repeating his phrase – trying to get a handle on it.

"We'll do everything," he said. "The license. The rings. The ceremony. And afterwards you'll get your green card and in three years you can get your citizenship. This way you can stay here and keep helping your family."

Not sure quite how to respond, Kara started voicing practical concerns.

"You could get in a lot of trouble if they find out. They could fine you, or send you to jail! And if they find out, they will deport me."

"Lovey, I can afford a fine, and if we don't do this, they'll deport you anyway!"

Kara quickly gave up on that line of objection. She felt deeply uncomfortable and surprisingly unhappy. But she knew, in reality, her negative emotions had nothing to do with a fear of getting caught. Rather, they came from the fact that the moment in front of her so closely resembled exactly what she wanted, yet was so crucially different from it.

Here was a man so unlike any other she had ever known. An ideal mate. Handsome, charming, witty, smart, wealthy. A man she was falling in love with. And he was asking to marry her. It would be a dream come true if it were real. But it wasn't. It was *fake*. It was for show. As much as she should have been jumping for joy at the opportunity he was offering her, she instead felt…pathetic.

"So you want to marry me?" she said. "But you don't want to marry me?"

"Look, Kara. We talked about this. I'm not the marrying type. I don't really want to settle down. I don't want to live with someone else full time. And I definitely don't want kids. You still want kids don't you?"

"Of course."

"You want a home and husband and a family right?"

"Yes. I do."

"I can't give you those things. But I can give you this. I can help you stay here. Kara, you don't deserve this. You're such a good person. You're sweet and kind. You take care of your patient and your family. You always put others before yourself."

At the moment, Kara felt selfish and did not fully agree with Dan's saint like description of her. But she did not interrupt it.

"You deserve the opportunities America has to offer," Dan continued. "If you want to stay I want to help you stay. I know I can't give you everything you want and I'm sorry about that. But I can give you this. Let me give you this."

Kara said nothing. She tried to think things through.

Dan held her hands tight.

"Also, I'll be honest," he said. "I don't want to lose you. Not yet."

"I don't want to lose you either," Kara said with a sigh.

"Great. So I'll ask you again." He got down on one knee. "Will you be my fake wife?"

"I don't know what to say," said Kara. She felt intensely conflicted. Rationally, she knew it was an opportunity she was not likely to have again. But emotionally she felt deeply opposed.

"Say yes!" implored Dan.

Kara stayed quiet.

Finally she said, "Can I have some time to think about it?"

"Of course," said Dan. He leaned over and kissed her. "Take as much time as you need."

Kara slipped into herself. She debated vigorously from within. She was caught in the crossfire between dreams and reality and she knew it would be impossible to escape unwounded.

# 7

"Is there anything else you need?" Kara said to Ramon, after bringing him his lunch.

"I am conflicted," Ramon said, after a pause.

"Hmmm?" said Kara

"Well I don't really want you to leave the room, but I so love watching you walk out."

Kara gave no signs of her usual revulsion to his vulgarity. In fact, she barely seemed to have heard him.

"That's it?" he said.

"What?"

"No reprimand? No grimace? Not even an eye roll?"

"To what?"

"Did you hear what I said?"

"What?"

"I said I don't really want you to leave the room, but I love watching you walk out."

"Oh," she said, faint, uninterested.

For the first time Ramon noticed how drained Kara seemed. He felt ashamed that he had paid so little attention to her.

"Kara, dear, what's the matter?" he asked.

"Nothing," she said, entirely unconvincingly.

"No. You're not your normal self. Something is wrong."

Kara stared at him. She looked like he was the last person in the world she wanted to talk to, but the worry which was eating away at her insides was so intense it was about to burst out on its own anyway.

"I am going to have to leave the country Ramon," she said.

"What? Why?"

"My visa is expiring."

"So renew it."

"I can't. I don't have a way. I've tried hard but there is no way."

Ramon became extremely incensed with this news.

"I don't understand," he said. "There must be something that can be done."

Kara went silent. She thought about Dan. She wasn't sure why she was so reluctant to bring him up. In a weird way she felt more pride in the idea of accepting her fate and returning home than in accepting Dan's pretend marriage proposal.

"I don't think so," said Kara.

"So I have to get another nurse?" said Ramon, completely indignant at the possibility.

"I'm afraid so," said Kara.

"But I don't want another nurse.'

"Thanks Ramon. But I am sure they'll find someone good in my place."

Ramon sighed. He saw her sadness and realized his own loss wasn't the primary concern here.

"I'm really sorry Kara. If there is anything I can do please let me know."

"I will. Thank you."

After a moment, Ramon broke the tension with a chuckle.

"Of course, if you want, I can always marry you and make you a citizen!" he said, almost entirely joking.

Kara was uncomfortable for a moment. Then she spotted the incredibly genuine look in the eyes of her patient. For all his inappropriateness, here was a man who really did care about her and her well-being. It was rather sweet.

"You are very kind to make that offer," she said. "Ramon, can I ask you a question?" she asked, after a moment of thoughtfulness.

"Of course my dear. Anything you'd like."

"Well…were you every married?"

"No. I was not."

"Engaged?"

"Nope."

"Ever come close? Sorry. It is too personal."

"Not at all. I had several serious relationships for sure. But I never got too close to marriage."

"How come?"

"It was just not for me. And while I love my nieces and nephews like they were my own, I never wanted any children. My brothers wanted the traditional family life, the wife and kids and all that, but it was never something I sought out."

Ramon paused. He looked uncharacteristically reflective. Kara wondered if he doubted his own words.

"I have no regrets. I'm happy with the way I lived my life."

"I see," said Kara.

"Of course," said Ramon, "If you want to take me up on my proposal, I won't turn you down!"

For a couple of days Kara's mind was so preoccupied that entire activities passed before her without a shred of conscious attention. She noticed herself on the bus ride home without any memory of having boarded the vehicle. She watched television programs and retained none of the storyline content when the end credits rolled. Most harmfully, she gave Ramon his pills and forgot whether she grouped the correct medicines together by the time she handed them to him. She prayed that she had automatically assorted the medication properly. Ramon's heart kept ticking so she figured everything must have been okay, but the incident struck her as very disturbing. She needed her mind back.

At night, in her apartment, she cuddled with Ricki and asked God for guidance. *Was it ever right to live a lie?*

Then she thought: *Would it be a lie?*

She did love Dan. Or at least, she was coming to. If he had asked her to marry him outright, without any stipulations, she would have said yes without any hesitation. The briefness of their courtship would have given her no pause.

But this mock marriage he was suggesting – the whole idea of it felt shameful. It wasn't really the violation of legal precedents which bothered her. (Though the notion of having to lie to the immigration officials was already a point of future anxiety). It wasn't necessarily the violation of moral code which caused her ache. (Though imagining what her grandmother say about such a flagrant violation of the Lord's sacred union gave her shudders). What really stung most of all was the violation of her pride.

*Am I not worthy of a real marriage?* she thought.

She felt pathetic and small. She knew Dan was doing the best he could, in his own way, to hold on to her. Yet she still felt somehow unwanted. Rejected. Not good enough for a real marriage rather than a sham one.

A part of her wanted to call Dan up right that second and throw his insult of a proposal right back in his face.

But another part of her knew she would never do that. Because she couldn't bear the thought of never seeing him again.

She couldn't bring herself to reject his offer. Yet she couldn't bring herself to accept it either. She felt torn and emotionally mangled from the inside out. She was frozen still in a coma of indecision.

The only person she wanted to talk to was Dan and he was the only person she couldn't talk to, since he was the subject of her dilemma.

So she prayed. And hoped God would give her the answer.

A couple of days later, she received one.

Kara's phone rang. It was her mother.

"Hola mama."

"Hola my sweet."

Kara could tell immediately that something was wrong. There was an uncharacteristic tremble in the typically cement solid voice of Maria.

"What is it?" Kara asked.

"It's your father," said Maria.

Kara went home as soon as she could.

While working on a construction job Juan had taken a nasty fall and broken his left arm and leg. He had also fractured his shoulder and bruised his entire side.

Kara found him at the hospital. Maria, Carmen, and Ricardo were all in the room looking grave. Though he had lost consciousness at the time of the accident, Juan was awake now and in a great deal of pain.

"Oh papa," Kara wailed, tears escaping, when she saw him.

She rushed over to his bed and took the hand of his unbroken arm.

"Hola my girl."

"What happened?"

Ricardo described the accident for her. He had been hammering nails into a floorboard on the second floor of a housing project when he had tripped over his own feet and fallen to the ground. He was lucky he hadn't broken his neck.

"Papa—" she said.

He cut her off.

"—I know Kara. I know. I am told. I cannot work anymore. It is too dangerous. I know, I know." He seemed disgusted with himself.

Kara hated seeing her father in such a position of vulnerability. He had always been a force of immovable strength in her life. It was shattering to see him broken in such a way – both physically and mentally. She pulled up a chair next to his bed and leaned her head on his pillow.

"I have done the best I could in the life," said Juan. "It's not always enough but it's the best I can do. I don't know what else to do but my best. I provided for my family. I did my best. For as long as I could. I did my best."

Juan started to cry. None of the children had ever seen their father shed a tear before. It was a harrowing sight.

Kara caught her mother's eye. Unspoken, they both acknowledged that Kara's money was needed more than ever.

And with that Kara realized her choice was no longer a choice. Her family needed her and she needed to do whatever was required to help them.

As soon as she left the hospital room, she called up Dan.

Dan was out at a bar with some friends when he felt his phone vibrate. When he saw Kara's name anticipatory goosebumps sailed up and down his body. He excused himself and hurried outside to answer the call before it went to voice mail.

"Hello," he said casually, as if he only answered the call because he had nothing better to do.

"Hi," said Kara.

"Hey sweetie. What's up?" said Dan, still severely overcompensating with nonchalance in trying not to sound nervous.

"I've thought about your proposal."

"Yes?"

Dan waited through an epically long pause (which in reality lasted only three seconds but felt like a hundred).

"I will accept. On one condition."

Dan felt relief flush through his body. The goosebumps settled. His lungs resumed churning air in and out of his nasal passages. He thought how amazing it was that he was getting so worked up about fake marriage proposal. He understood the irony of the moment, but he couldn't help feeling extremely happy that she had said yes.

"Of course," he said. "Anything."

"I want you to come down to Tijuana and ask my father for permission."

Dan almost laughed. If he didn't know Kara better he might have thought it was a joke.

"You want me to ask your father's permission to have a green card marriage with you?"

"Yes. Well no. I want you to ask his permission to marry me. To pretend it's real."

"You want to lie to your parents?"

"I'm going to have to anyway."

"Why?"

"They will need to know how I was able to stay in the States. And it would bring my father too much shame to think that I was committing a crime to stay."

"It's not a crime—"

"My father would be greatly honored if you would ask for my hand."

Dan felt a wave of resistance.

"Kara, I don't know..."

"Please Dan. It would mean a lot to me."

Dan stopped for a moment to step out of his own body and look at his current situation as if he was an objective observer.

Sitting in the bar, waiting for him, were two of his closest and oldest friends, Brian and Lance. Both were married. Both had children. Both were, at times, miserable with their situations. Both were, at other times, quite happy – or so they said, though Dan mostly heard complaints. For years they had both tried to convince Dan of the merits of marriage. For years Dan had shrugged off their pestering, which seemed to be backed up by little concrete day to day evidence. He laughed, defiant of their dissonant, misguided interpretations of their own emotions, filtered through the necessity of justification. He had watched Lance brush against the possibility of divorce in a particularly tense period in his marriage after he and his spouse had been mutually unfaithful to one another; yet still praise the institution of marriage to Dan after he had reconciled with his wife.

Dan felt the same way he always had about getting married. He had no desire to link himself to Kara on any permanent basis and he was sure that doing so would lead to nothing but unhappiness for the both of them.

But there he was – contrary to all his rational thoughts – prepared to do anything it took to gain the girl on the other end of the phone's fictional hand in marriage. Overjoyed, in fact, at the thought of exchanging vows with her – temporary though they might be.

"Lovey, if it makes you happy," he said, "I'll drive down there right now."

He drove down a week later. Kara was with him.

On Friday, while she was still back in Los Angeles tending to Ramon, Juan was moved back home from the hospital. He was given strict orders not to move too fast or bend down too far or lift anything too heavy, but he was at least allowed to sleep in his own bed and be with his family.

His spirits were given a nice lift when he was informed that Kara was coming to visit with a man she had been seeing. He was very excited to meet Dan.

Yet when they arrived, Juan thought it only proper to play the role of strict, concerned father. Thus, the expression that Dan saw on Juan's face when they shook hands was not an excited smile, but rather a determined grimace featuring a small chance of homicide.

Entering the Gomez family compound, a few thoughts ran through Dan's head. One, although the family certainly wasn't overflowing with money, their living space wasn't nearly as third world as Dan (now he thought, somewhat racistly, or at least xenophobically) pictured in his mind. Tijuana – which he had only previously seen via dance clubs and bars on a drunken, hazy weekend in his youth – had more to it than endless squalor. Sure many of the roads were paths of sandy dirt rather than paved asphalt streets, but there was still reason for the city's residents to have pride in their homes, even if little affluence was to be found.

Another thought was that walking into the midst of the Gomez family gave Dan some impression of what an animal in a zoo must feel like. A great deal of the extended clan had apparently been invited (or, as he later found out, invited themselves) to come ogle the rare, openly presented man in sweet Kara's life. Everyone in the room stared openly at him without awkwardness or hesitation. There were smiles on their faces and threats in their eyebrows. They welcomed him openly with joy, while ready to claw into him should any evidence of harm to Kara present itself.

Dan was introduced to all of the relatives, receiving one delighted hug after another. He met Maria and Ricardo. He met her grandmother Rosita. He met her cousins Adriana, Martha, and Margarita who swooned like groupies. He met Carmen, who didn't even bother to wait until Dan was out of sight to tell Kara (in Spanish) that he was a looker. Dan knew enough of the language to understand the compliment and respond with a courteous "gracias."

Finally, at the kitchen table, waiting like the judge in his high seat, was Juan. Dan introduced himself, traded a finger crushing handshake and sat down at the table with Kara.

Kara swore later that she had not given any advance warning to anyone in her family of the reason for her visit, but when Dan sat down on the table the room went silent with eager anticipation. They all watched, waiting for the show.

Dan was someone who could speak in front of a crowd of hundreds about financial advice without an ounce of nervous sweat escaping his skin. Not a jangle of worry hit him before stepping out on a stage in front of a giant hall of eyes, all focused on him. At the moment, however, he could feel his armpit glands go into overdrive and his heart start to pound. He hyperbolically thought that this was the most uncomfortable he had ever felt in his entire life.

Perhaps the tension he felt was due to his looming dishonesty. During his conferences, he always felt he was presenting those who had paid to see him with the most truthful account of his expertise that he could. He had even made a sticking point of continuing to be honest when he joined the financial network. But this moment...this was an act. He had to perform in a way he never did in any of his usual work. And the audience watching him looked ready to throw tomatoes and hook him off stage at the first flubbed line.

He looked over at Kara. She seemed just as wrapped up in watching him as everyone else in the room. More nervous though. She would be no comfort to him right now. He was on his own.

"Mr. Gomez," he said.

The ears of everyone in the room perked up like wolves hearing their prey rustle in the bushes.

Juan said nothing. He just continued to look at Dan like he was a bug to be crushed at the first wrong word.

"I came here today," Dan continued, "to ask for your permission to ask for your daughter's hand in marriage."

Juan leaned slowly forward. His chair creaked imposingly. Everyone else in the room leaned in along with him.

"Are you into drugs?" asked Juan.

The question was so unexpected that Dan almost laughed, but luckily he restrained himself.

"I am not sir," he said.

"Do you have a good job? Can you give things to my daughter?"

"I do sir. I can sir."

"Tell me about this job."

"I am a financial expert. I have a radio show in California and I appear on a television channel based in New York."

Juan looked impressed for a moment, before he wiped any joy from his face.

"I could use some financial advice," blurted out Manuel, Kara's first cousin. The entire room turned to look at him with condescension. Juan told Manuel to shut his mouth with a flick of the eyebrow, then turned back to Dan.

"Will you be faithful to Kara?" he asked.

"Always," said Dan.

"Do you want children?"

Dan hesitated for only the slightest section. Although he didn't really believe in ESP, he hoped that no one in the room was a psychic.

"Of course," he answered.

He caught Kara's eye. He thought he saw a split second look of deep sadness.

Juan turned to his daughter as well. As soon as he did, she put a smile on her face.

"Is he a good man?" Juan asked her.

"He is," Kara said with complete conviction.

"Do you love him?"

"Yes."

"Do you want to marry him?"

"I do," she said, just as truthfully as she answered the previous questions.

The harsh judgment on Juan's face suddenly broke like a long night abruptly interrupted by the rising sun.

He smiled and Dan at once saw the charming man who Kara loved so dearly.

"Then Daniel, you have my permission and blessing. Congratulations."

Juan shook Dan's hand once more. The grip was just as tight, but this time Dan felt loved instead of threatened.

"Thank you Mr. Gomez. Thank you."

Now that the most profound tension was over, Dan felt his usual room leading confidence return in full force. Everyone in the household had taken a collective breath upon Juan's declared approval, but they also all seemed to be waiting for something more to occur. Dan figured there was no point in any further delay. The family wanted a show and he would give them one.

He stood up with purpose, grabbed Kara's hand, and led her out of the crowded kitchen.

Everyone else hurriedly followed like Dan was Moses and they needed to make it across the red sea before the waves closed back upon them. He didn't know where he was going, but he easily found the door to the backyard and ushered Kara outdoors with a gleeful trot.

He allowed a few moments for his audience to form a ritualistic circle around him and Kara. He looked into the eyes of the woman he had agreed to put on this show for. Her expression was hard to read. She looked blank. He took it for nervousness.

Once he gathered that everyone had made it into the yard, he got down on one knee and pulled a small leather box out of his pocket. He opened it. Inside was a rather expensive looking engagement ring featuring a diamond the size of a small grape.

Kara gasped. Now Dan could read her expression. Intense surprise. Apparently she didn't expect such an extravagant ornament for their "fake" marriage. She underestimated him.

"Kara Gomez," he said, "will you marry me?"

Kara smiled. For the first time in a few weeks, unrestrained joy came over her. At least for a moment.

"Yes. I will marry you," she said.

Dan jumped up and slid the engagement ring on Kara's finger. He pulled her in for a passionate kiss. The Gomez clan erupted in cheers.

It wasn't long before a heaping of neighbors and yet more of Kara's family made their way over, somehow having heard the news, and a full, unplanned party was in swing. Maria went straight to work as cooking maestro, directing various cousins and children in a symphony of food gathering and preparation. A delicious aroma engulfed the place in no time.

Now unofficially a member of the family, Dan was the star attraction of the event. He was swamped by a long line of interviewers, wishing to learn more about the mysterious rich American who was going to marry their Kara. He was not even immune to the intense interviewing of five year old Carlos, accompanied by his father Jorge.

Carlos's interview involved no words. He just walked over to Dan and stared at him.

"Hi there," said Dan. "What's your name?"

Carlos continued to stare. Dan looked to Jorge.

"Does he understand English?" he asked.

"He does. Sorry." said Jorge. "Carlos, say hello to your new Uncle Dan."

Carlos continued to peer into Dan's eyes without a word. Then he abruptly ran away.

Kara received her fair share of attention as well, but Dan was the party's superstar and Kara was glad for it. She didn't want to be watched too closely. She was afraid that her thinly constructed exterior might crumble and her family might see the real emotions hiding inside.

For one small moment on that bizarre, uncomfortable day she had felt real happiness. And that true feeling of happiness was a moment of delirious fantasy. It was a brief instance of being lost in a dream and falsely believing it to be real.

Right when Dan opened his ring and stated his proposal, for a brief moment, Kara believed – truly believed – that it was all real and she had finally met the man with whom she would spend the rest of her life. A delirious surge of pleasure swam up and down her body and the cheers of her family were the white noise of perfection. It must have been the gleam of the diamond in her eyes, piercing to her brain and causing her to forget reality, because just as quick the true facts of the situation fell back down upon her. She wanted to run. Far away. But she could not. This half-truth of a temporary marriage was now to be her life.

While Jorge and Carlos "talked" with Dan, Kara stole a brief moment of solitude for herself inside the house, which was quickly interrupted by Carmen.

"I've got to hand it to you little sister," she said, "That is one good looking Gringo."

Kara forced a smile.

"I'm very impressed. I guess all that talk about him not being the marrying type was not too serious."

"I guess."

"Or maybe you just really turned on the charm. Did you give him some things he cannot get anywhere else?" said Carmen suggestively.

Kara just shrugged her shoulders. It was too much, trying to pretend she was happy in front of her bluntly honest sister. She felt tears coming on.

"And there's going to be a wedding! I cannot wait. You're going to need a wedding dress. I have this friend—"

Kara could not hold back any longer. Her tears burst through.

Carmen misinterpreted the sobbing as joyful and shook her head with sisterly sarcasm.

"Sweetheart I know you're happy but this is entirely unnecessarily," she said with an ironic flair.

Kara threw her arms around Carmen for a tight hug. She rested her head on her shoulder.

She forced the words out.

"Sorry. I'm just…so…happy," she said, hiding her face so Carmen couldn't parse out the truth.

"I know you are honey," said Carmen, rubbing Kara on the back with affection.

Right then, Dan walked in the room. He had managed to escape his press junket of introductory interviews in order to find his "fiancée."

He stopped still when he saw Kara crying.

Carmen shook her head towards him.

"Look what you've done to my sister," she said.

"What?" he said, concerned.

"You have made her far too happy. She cannot even function."

Dan looked closely at Kara who was avoiding his eyes. She was not happy. He could tell that much.


Dan and Kara didn't speak much before the car ride home. He decided to let her feel whatever she was feeling and not pressure her to open up while they were with her family.

After they hugged everyone goodbye and got into his Mercedes to drive back to Los Angeles, Dan planned to have the kind of emotionally charged, inevitably highly conflicted relationship conversation that he usually avoided at all costs. He felt it was probably his duty to ask Kara what was going on in her head.

The start of the car ride was filled with suffocating silence and Dan quickly realized he was not going to initiate the conversation that he planned to. He couldn't bring himself to do it.

Dan had originally had the idea to offer Kara a green card marriage because he loved spending time with her and didn't want to let her go yet. But ever since his proposal most of their time spent together or talking with each other had been filled with distance and tension. It was giving him doubts about the whole thing, but it was certainly too late to take back his offer. What he really wanted was the real Kara back. Not this quiet, moody girl who had been swapped for her. He didn't want to have a stressed couple's argument. He wanted to enjoy his time with this girl. He wanted to reclaim the glory which had led him here in the first place.

Dan had an idea.

"Lovey," he said, breaking the long silence, "I have one word for you."

"Yes?" she said.

"Hawaii," said Dan.

Kara waited for a moment for more. She had no idea what he was getting at. Dan just smiled.

"Hawaii?" she asked.

"Hawaii," he said again, with even more confidence.

"What about it?"

"Let's get married there."

"My family cannot afford to go to Hawaii."

"They wouldn't be there. It would just be the two of us. Married on a beach in paradise all by ourselves."

Kara was about to respond negatively when she stopped herself and thought over his suggestion. If it was a real marriage she was entering into, she would have been insulted by the suggestion that her family be ignored completely in favor of a private ceremony. But the truth was, she was worried about keeping up her performance of glee in front of her loved ones anyway. Having an isolated island ceremony might actually be the best thing for her. She wouldn't have to spend the whole day lying. She could relax and accept her and Dan's vows for what they really were: a temporary agreement.

Hawaii. It would be incredibly gorgeous. She and Dan could have fun there. They could get back to the people they really were. They could resume their romance. At least for a little while.

"Hawaii," she said. "Yes. Maybe this is a good idea."

Hawaii was even more beautiful and luxurious than Kara could have hoped. Dan booked them a suite at the Ritz Carlton hotel, right on the beach in Maui. The hotel was filled with golden chandeliers and plush hallway carpets and acres of pools and white cloth tabled restaurants with large windows overlooking the ocean. The room was modern and decadent. The island was breathtaking with its pristine beaches and blue water, so different from the green gray color of the Pacific on the California coast.

The picturesque change of scenery felt like a long delayed breath of air to a relationship which had been submerged under water for a bit too long.

Kara felt momentarily relaxed. The decision was made. The marriage was happening. They were alone and there was no pressure to please anyone but themselves. If Dan wanted to call an end to things at some point down the road that was out of her control, but in the meantime she might as well try to enjoy it.

When they entered the suite, she threw down her bags and threw her arms and legs around Dan.

"Well hi there," he said.

"Hello."

She kissed him passionately.

"This is nice," she said. "Thank you for taking me here."

"The pleasure is all mine."

It was late and they were exhausted from the long flight. They settled in and were both quickly sound asleep.

The next day was the wedding.

On the recommendation of a friend, Dan planned the ceremony for a secluded cove of a beach in Wailea. He rented a Jeep and with their suit and gown in tow, they made their way to the beach.

A priest and a photographer were to meet them there. Dan insisted that photos would be necessary to show the USCIS officials, in order to prove the validity of the marriage. Thinking of the inevitable future inquiry sent a swift rush of terror up and down Kara's spine. She let the emotions recede quickly. She was nervous enough about the imminent marriage ceremony. She didn't want to ruin her day thinking about events off in the distance.

Kara stared out the window at the passing wonder as Dan drove along the coastal road. In a reflective mood, she thought of her place in nature and her mysterious connection with all else in existence.

Dan parked his car on a curved patch of sand which doubled as a parking lot for the isolated beach. Two other cars were already parked there.

"Alright," said Dan. "Let's get hitched."

They got out and Kara looked around. A burst of panic descended upon her.

"Dan, there's nowhere to change."

Dan looked around casually.

"Huh, you're right."

Kara did not think his tone carried nearly enough urgency. He sounded like a man about to spend a leisurely day sunbathing, not one about to be the groom in what was technically a criminal wedding which could end in deportation and jail time if everything wasn't done with the utmost precision.

"Oh well," said Dan.

He reached behind him and pulled his suit bag off the hook. He pulled his shirt over his head and unzipped the bag.

"What are you doing!?" said Kara, with the maximum shock she could infuse into her statement.

"Changing," said Dan calmly.

"But—but—"

"Relax Lovey. No one is around. We were the only car on the road."

"What about those?" she said indicating the other vehicles in the parking lot.

"That's probably the priest and the photographer. They must be out on the beach already."

Dan took off his pants. Kara buried her face in her hands. Dan slipped on the remainder of his suit.

"Alright Lovey," he said. "It's your turn."

Kara looked around, mortified. Committing a criminal act was one thing. Disrobing in public was another issue entirely.

"Kara, you can't get married in shorts and a tank top," he said, genuinely sounding surprised at how hard of a time she was having with this.

"I can't change in the seat like you can," she said. "I need more space."

"Okay."

Dan got out of the car and opened the trunk. He pulled out a beach towel and laid it on the ground next to the car.

"There, I promise I won't look," he said.

Kara shook her head, resigned herself to the situation, and stepped out of the car. She stripped down to her underwear, constantly peeking back at the road, praying no one would drive by. She did the hard work of sliding into her slim white wedding dress as swiftly as her body would allow.

"Okay," she said, when she felt she was properly arranged. She took a relieved breath that no cars had passed.

Dan turned around and looked at her. His eyes went wide.

"Wow, you look amazing," he said, with a hundred percent conviction, not a trace of the automatic in his compliment.

Kara blushed. "Thanks," she said.

"Are you Mr. McCoy and Miss Gomez?" said a voice a few feet away, surprising them with its sudden appearance.

They looked up. Watching them from a collection of rocks which led to the beach path were a middle aged priest and photographer in his twenties smiling a large, awkward grin.

"We are," said Dan. He waited a moment, then asked, "How long have you been standing there?"

The priest looked down awkwardly. The photographer extended his awkward smile. "Uh…not long…" he said unconvincingly.

Dan looked at Kara with an apologetic smirk.

"They saw everything!" said Kara, partly embarrassed, partly vindicated that she was correct in her concern.

"Yes. Yes they did," said Dan, conceding the argument. "Sorry," he said sheepishly, then started laughing.

As embarrassed as Kara was, now that nothing could be done about the situation she saw the humor in it. Or at least, she saw why Dan would find it funny. He did delight her, this man – even in his profound differences from her. His laughter was contagious. She started to laugh herself and leaned her head against his arm. He kissed her.

The priest and the photographer shared a look. Unspoken, they wondered just what kind of nuts they were dealing with.

Out on the sand, Dan and Kara chose a spot to conduct the ceremony. They faced away from the ocean so that the bright blue water would appear in their pictures. Dan placed his battery powered ipod speaker system on the ground and asked the photographer if he would do him the favor of pressing play when the moment was right. "Every girl deserves to walk to 'Here Comes the Bride' on her wedding day," he said.

When everything was in place, Kara disappeared behind a set of palm trees.

The brief levity of laughing with Dan vanished and she was greeted once more with the painful uncertainty and moral distress of her situation. She had never known that truth and lies could become so entangled into such an unrecognizable mixture.

A million thoughts ran through her head. She said her prayer to God, asking for guidance.

Then she re-emerged to set things in motion.

She slowly walked up to the man she had not known just four months before. A man who she would now be forever tied to in one way or another. He looked fulfilled. Happy.

Kara felt hopeful.

The young photographer snapped photos busily. Dan motioned to him to turn off the music. The priest kindly smiled at Kara. If there were any signs of falseness to the proceedings he could not see them.

When the ipod clicked to silence, the priest began his speech.

"We are here today to join these two souls together in holy matrimony…" he said.

Kara missed most of what he had to say, lost in a fog looking at Dan's eyes, her heart beating a million miles an hour. She tuned in for the final bit.

"Kara do you take this man to be your lawfully wedded husband? To have and to hold from this day forward; for better or for worse; for richer or for poorer; in sickness and in health; to love and to cherish for as long as you both shall live?"

Kara gulped. Time to dive off the cliff and hope there weren't jagged rocks below.

"I do," she said.

She looked at the sky. No lightning bolts. No condemnation from God. It was done. Now what would be would be. Dan smiled at her. She smiled back.

"Dan, do you take this woman to be your lawfully wedded wife? To have and to hold from this day forward; for better or for worse; for richer or for poorer; in sickness and in health; to love and to cherish for as long as you both shall live?"

"I do," said Dan, confidently. Not even a blink at his half truth.

Kara's suppressed happiness grew.

"Then by the power vested in me, I now pronounce you husband and wife," said the priest. "You may now kiss the bride."

Dan swept her into his arms, powerfully. They locked lips passionately. The photographer's flash bulbs went off like the supernatural lightning storm Kara feared for her transgressions.

After dispensing with the legal paperwork with the priest (using the photographer as their witness) the eager young portrait taker swept the newlyweds up for a proper posed photo session against the picturesque backdrop.

Young and idealistic, eager to squeeze perfection out of each image, the photographer molded them like plaster figurines into the exact poses he visualized in his mind. He even went so far as to tell them to pretend to be in mid-laugh for a sculpted "candid."

Kara went along with the orders like the compulsive rule follower she often hated being, but Dan quickly got fed up and decided to take control of the situation.

"That's enough of that, I think," said Dan, after he and Kara posed back to back like members of Charlie's Angels. "Let's do something more fun."

Abruptly, he backed up to Kara and hoisted her onto his back. She let out a little yelp of surprise, though she was actually delighted with his rather masculine display of playful aggression.

"This way," Dan said to the photographer.

Dan ran with Kara down the beach as she screamed and laughed in perfect symmetrical unison. The photographer snapped away, amazed that images of such joy could occur without his precise direction.

After a nice jog, he put her down and she lightheartedly hit him on the arm.

"Naughty," she said, as if she had actually been bothered by his manhandling.

That word was enough to turn him on right then and there. If it weren't for the fact that a photographer and a priest were watching he might not have been able to hold back. As it was, he pulled Kara in and kissed her intensely, dipping her back like a nineteen-forties dame.

That night Dan took Kara to the most expensive restaurant he could find.

Dan ordered a hundred dollar bottle of wine. He looked at Kara and said: "Sorry babe, it's your wedding night, so no milk for you."

"Oh, alright," she said, as if she would have done anything but exactly what Dan said at that moment.

Kara was in a terrific mood. She could physically feel the mostly unspoken tension which had existed between them for the past couple of weeks melt away.

Dan had not mentioned it but she knew he had quickly become tired of her mixed feelings at his proposal. Overall he had been extremely patient. He had been kind and understanding and he had never rescinded his offer. All the same, he kept speaking to her like she was some guard against her own enjoyment, keeping the real Kara under lock and key. She was delighted to see the relief in his eyes when, now that the ceremony was over, she shredded her outer layer of disappointment and decided to just enjoy things for what they were.

When the wine arrived, Dan raised his glass.

"To us," he said.

"To us," Kara replied, fully in the moment – forgetting all her cares for just one night.

"To a perfect honeymoon," he said.

For a moment Kara couldn't help but remember Carmen's remark that Dan wanted "just the honeymoon." It struck her as an incredibly accurate insight. Dan was only interested in the fun part of a relationship, she knew. He had no interested in fighting through a lifetime of good and bad times. "For better or for worse," the priest had said. Dan had agreed but it was a lie. He had no intention of sticking around for "the worse." His basic refusal to commit to experiencing the bad that came with the good was frustrating. But it was also what made Dan who he was. His preference for embracing the positive and avoiding the negative was part of what made him so appealing.

"To the honeymoon," she replied happily, glad to share this moment in time with this man, regardless of what would happen later.

As they ate and drank and got a little drunk, they chatted and laughed and flirted and everything seemed just as it should be.

Dan, in a terrific mood, left an overly generous tip and led Kara by hand out of the restaurant. They took a taxi back to the hotel and could barely wait to get to their hotel room before ripping each other's clothes off. They just made it.

Dan woke up the next morning with Kara in his arms.

His left hand was tucked under her head and was completely numb from having been lodged there for the evening. The pins and needles were intense but he had no intention of waking the beautiful sleeping girl who held his hand captive.

As a general principle Dan hated thinking about his own future. Other people's futures were a different story. What he did for a living was to predict how financial situations would unfold over time. Thinking about that gave him no stress. On the contrary – it gave him great pleasure. But perhaps that was because he felt confident in being able to predict how the finances would change and grow and lessen. His own personal life was far less easy to prophesize. The payoff was also far less satisfying. A correct prediction of stocks led to a larger bank account. A correct prediction of a relationship led to annoyance, frustration, and loneliness. Better to not look too far ahead. Otherwise he would risk missing all the good parts.

Still, sometimes there were things that had to be thought about. There were things that had to be discussed. There was an important conversation with Kara he had put off for longer than he should have. He certainly should have brought it up before they actually tied the knot, but he supposed he hoped the legal tie might keep them bound together at least until things started to go sour. This morning was the time. He could not put off the conversation any longer.

Kara slowly woke up as he watched her. She smiled before she opened her eyes. She looked like she was moving from a great dream to an even better reality.

"Good morning," she said, in that accent Dan so enjoyed hearing.

"Good morning Miss Gomez," he said.

"Mrs. McCoy," she said, her eyes closed once more.

"Are you taking my name?" he asked, genuinely surprised. It had not occurred to him she might want to.

She shrugged. "Maybe I have not decided yet."

She was in a good mood this morning. Dan was thrilled to see that her happiness had not worn off along with the alcohol.

"I love you," he blurted out. His rational side though it was a stupid thing to say. But it was undoubtedly what he felt.

"I love you too Daniel." She leaned in and kissed him.

"I'm sorry you couldn't have your family here," he said. "I know how close you are with them."

"It was easier," she said, hugging her pillow tight, thoroughly wrapped up in the bed and the moment – the deepest of physical and emotional comfort merged into one gooey motionless meld. "Did you care that your family was not here?"

A brief jolt of panic exploded in Dan like a miniature stress big bang. He regained his composure quickly enough that Kara would not spot the intrusion. He finally pulled his numb hand out from under her so it could regain some life. With his other hand he brushed her hair out of her eyes. Then he moved his fingers to her side and rubbed her skin gently.

*Do I really want to go into this right now?*, he thought to himself. *She is my wife*, his mind answered.

"I don't have any family," he said.

"I thought you said you had two sisters," she said, still restful, not yet having realized the conversation had transitioned from morning-after chit-chat into something more serious.

"I did. I did have two sisters. Now I only have one and we don't speak."

Kara opened her eyes fully. She propped herself up on her pillow.

"I'm so sorry Daniel. What happened?"

Dan breathed in a big gulp of fresh air. He had opened the door on the topic. His instinct was to back away but he knew it was too late for that. This wasn't even the serious conversation he intended on having with Kara that morning, but just like that, with little warning, he was submerged once again in his life's tragic moments.

"My little sister, Holly, she had cancer. Pancreatic. Really hard to diagnose early and really hard to cure. She died."

Kara's beautiful face twisted with sorrow. She put her hand on Dan's cheek.

"Oh my love. I'm so sorry."

"Thanks. It was…" Dan stopped himself. He realized he was about to cry. It had been so long since he had shed a tear, it really took him by surprise. Holly's death was mostly a cold, unchangeable fact to him now. But he so rarely talked to another person about it and he was in such an emotionally vulnerable position at the moment that tears made a long delayed return to the back of his eyes. He took a moment to compose himself. He tried to force the watery discharge back where it came from. After a little effort and a hard grip of his hand by Kara's fingers, it seemed to work.

"It was really hard," he said. "She was still so young and full of promise. The truth is things have never been the same since then."

Dan did not elaborate on his statement, but he knew it was true. His sister's death had changed him. *And maybe not for the better*, he thought, harshly.

"Both of my parents died when I was young," he said, not going into the details. "My oldest sister and I were already somewhat isolated from each other so when Holly died we just sort of stopped talking." He didn't mention Rebecca. He didn't want to talk about ex-girlfriends with Kara. At least not right then.

"I know I should reach out to her," he said. "But the truth is it's easier not to."

Kara said nothing at first. She took in this new information. She wondered if all of the loss in Dan's life was the reason he didn't want marriage and children. If he was too afraid of more loss. She decided it would be best not to voice these possible psychological insights out loud.

"You should talk to her," Kara said. "Family is important."

Dan said nothing. He just shrugged his shoulders as if there was nothing to be done about the situation.

"I lost someone as well," she eventually said. "Teresa. She was my best friend. She died four years ago."

"Oh. I'm sorry to hear that Lovey."

Kara nodded in appreciation at his condolences.

The newlyweds spent a long silent moment looking in each other's eyes. Independently, it occurred to each of them how little they actually knew about each other. Their time together, all told, had been brief. Their deep, revealing conversations had been minimal. There was an immense amount of mystery hidden beneath the surface and they had only glimpsed the very tip of the iceberg of each other's selves.

Dan thought about how little you ever learn about another person; how much always remained hidden from view no matter how close you got.

Kara wondered whether their whole relationship was just based on mutually agreed fantasies. She wondered if there was actually anything real to it at all.

"Kara, I really care about you," Dan said. "I want you to know that. No matter what happens, I really want to do what's best for you. I feel comfortable telling you things about myself because I trust you. And I want you to know I am going to do everything I can to make sure you have a good life in America."

"Thanks Daniel."

"Look, there's something I need to say to you. Something I've been meaning to say."

"Yes?"

Kara felt tense. She wasn't sure what was coming.

"This is not easy for me to say, but I also feel like I can't spend another minute with you without getting it off my chest."

"Okay." She was desperate for him to spit out whatever he was going to say.

"I am going to be with you throughout this whole legal process and afterwards. I want this to continue the way it's been for as long as you would like it to. But I also don't want to deny you what you really want... What I want to say is— if you find someone and he can give you what I can't, I want you to feel free to be with him. Date him. Spend time with him. Do what you need to do for you. Don't worry about me. If you connect with anyone and you want to give him a shot, I think you should do it."

All of Kara's muscles tightened muscles relaxed as Dan finished speaking but she still felt deeply confused.

*I do not understand this man*, she thought profoundly. *Not even a little bit.* She understood in a lifeless detached way that Dan felt certain he didn't want marriage or children. At the same time, he seemed full of love and devotion for her. It was hard for her to reconcile the impassioned man in front of her with the non-committal man. As much as she wanted to accept him for who he said he was, truthfully it was hard for her to understand his position on romance.

"Are you sure?" she said.

"Yes," he said, not remotely sounding sure. "If you're happy, I'm happy."

Kara nodded. "Okay," she said.

Then she promptly did her best to put everything he said out of her mind.

"Come here," she said, seductively directing him on top of her.

Everything he talked about was all so *theoretical*. She would let Dan be certain about their doomed future. As for her, she would just wait and see.

# PART III:
## SEPTEMBER 2013 - JANUARY 2014

# 8

Raul Salazar pulled up to the house of the woman who was now officially his ex-wife, forced to say what was now a routine goodbye to his children. For the remainder of their childhood Nick and Elizabeth would be passed back and forth between their parents. Accepting that this pattern was the new normal didn't make it any easier for Raul to bear. Seeing the look on little Lizzie's face, unable to completely comprehend the circumstances of her parents' separation, broke his heart every time. Eleven year old Nick's full understanding might have been even worse. Lizzie at least possessed an unrealistic hope that things might get back to normal. Nick showed no such optimism and his resignation was devastating.

"Do you guys have anything fun planned this week?" asked Raul, delaying the parting for as long as possible.

"No," said Nick. The boy had become increasingly moody as of late. Raul was very concerned that his son would be one of those children who suffered irreparable psychological damage as a result of his parents' divorce – spiraling downward into poor grades and bad behavior and drug use and eventual jail time. *It's hard not to have your worries wander to the most extreme possibility when you're a parent,* thought Raul.

His daughter was more verbose with her answer.

"Mommy said she's going to take us to the mall and the movies and the beach," said Lizzie.

Raul felt himself get angry for no reason. Just hearing the word "mommy" from his daughter's lips was enough to trigger petty feelings of irritation and resentment.

Raul never expected to be someone who would suffer a bitter, heated divorce. Of course no one ever expects to get divorced when they get married – otherwise they would never commit in the first place. One hundred percent of people feel they will end up in the positive fifty percent of the statistics. Even now, Raul didn't blame himself or anyone else for ignoring the mathematical probabilities of the situation. *You have to believe a relationship is going to work or else it has no chance of working*, he thought. *Full confidence is required even if you are doomed to failure.* He and Nicole were apparently doomed to failure. Or, at least, they did fail. Whether or not they were fated to do so from the very beginning was something he would never know.

Yet, somehow, it wasn't the divorce itself that shocked and upset him as much as the truly terrible nature of how things went down.

There was no specific smoking gun. No glaring act of betrayal by one party that swiftly tore the coupling apart and cleanly filtered them into "good guy" and "bad guy" boxes for the public eye and the clarity of their own guilt complexes. The end was slow and painful. A bullet to the stomach that bled out gradually instead of a swift shot to the head.

All of the little, forgivable quirks that Raul and Nicole didn't particularly love about each other when they got together, but were willing to look past, didn't seem so easy to ignore after several years of marriage. At first they complained about one another subtly, under the pretext that it was teasing from a place of love.

Raul's tendency to wolf down large bits of food in quick inhaling successions of two or three bites at one time made Nicole playfully laugh about Raul's "masculine untamed appetite." When things got more testy, she started accusing him of lapping up his food in a more disgusting manner than Rufus, the family dog. At one point she gave Raul a plate of dog food for dinner with a malicious smile and no apparent actual meal to exchange it with when the joke had run its course. She began to comment excessively on the few extra pounds on him, which she originally called "love handles," and she now unceremoniously called his "fat." Anytime someone outside of the family was around she would make a point of joking that she couldn't see them around Raul's stomach. Feeling self-conscious about his physique (which, all told wasn't *that* overweight – just a little pudgy) he started to exercise in the house, lifting weights and attempting short bursts of push-ups and sit-ups. His efforts only gained him more derision. She seemed to find his attempts at fitness funnier than any sitcom on television.

Raul was no saint with Nicole either. Fully aware that she was overly self-conscious about not becoming her mother, who had always been overbearing and demanding with her children, Raul made a point of calling attention to any slight wording or action in which Nicole resembled her parent. He did so under the excuse that she had said, "don't ever let me become that woman," on one of their first evenings spent with her parents. It got to the point where she could barely discipline their children without an irritating "tsk-tsk," from Raul's corner of the room. He was fully aware of how obnoxious he was being but didn't bother to stop, finding her annoyance increasingly hilarious.

Then, as time went on, the humorous tone of mocking wore off more and more until a harsh, fragile undercoating of *dislike* was discovered.

They were no longer lovers walking the tight rope of mean-spirited flirtation. They were competitors in a heated debate trying to expose each other's fallacies to a non-existent audience.

She yelled at him, calling him dull, dumb, and pathetic.

He fired back, accusing her of being cold and micromanaging.

She said that he was increasingly unattractive.

He said that she was boring in bed.

She said good, because she had no desire to be crushed under his weight during sex anymore anyway.

It got to the point where they had no other interaction but screaming. They both knew it was horrible for the children, hiding one room away from their parents' raised voices and horrible cutting words. But they were powerless to stop it. Their hate for each other was a bubbling chemical interaction. They were too caught up in its frothy explosion to step back and start to clean up the mess.

Eventually, a divorce became inevitable. When Nicole finally threw the d-word out there, there was not a hint of surprise on Raul's part. Actually, he wondered why one of them hadn't brought it up sooner. It made him question whether they had been thriving on their battles in some way. It was too dark a line of thinking for him to consider for long. Talking about divorce, he was the calmest he had been with her in months. He agreed to her request and the legal separation swiftly got under way.

As the papers were signed and the assets were split, Raul looked back and tried to find where exactly things went so terribly wrong. There had to be a specific turning point, he thought. He searched and filed through his memories but no particular instance came to mind. That bothered him almost as much as anything. He wanted an incident to blame and he located no such comfort.

After saying goodbye to his kids, Raul drove down to his Uncle Ramon's house. It had been a couple months since he last stopped by and he owed his Uncle a visit.

Raul's enjoyment of Ramon's company depended on his particular mood. If he was feeling happy, or even mildly pleasant, Ramon delighted him with his unapologetic chauvinism and his know-it-all intensity, which had not lessened in the least with the decline of his physical faculties. However, if Raul was feeling dejected or bitter (as he did the vast majority of the time in the months following his divorce) his Uncle's blunt questions and unmannered outspokenness came off as extremely obnoxious and made Raul want to throw one of the mansion's many ceramic objects against the wall.

Thus, Raul had mostly been avoiding his uncle as of late.

The longer he went without a visit, the guiltier he felt and eventually his guilt outweighed the prospect of unpleasantness.

Raul was Ramon's only real family. Raul was the only child of deceased parents and Ramon was the childless brother of his late father. Ramon and Raul Sr. had other siblings who had other children but none of them made any effort to see Ramon. They all said they found him unpleasant. Raul was the only one who bothered to visit. He was the only one who cared.

His uncle may have made a show of loudly declaring his Ayn Rand inspired self-reliance, but Raul knew he craved human contact as much as anyone else. He saw Ramon's eyes light up when he showed up unexpectedly at the house.

So even though he was not at all in the mood for a visit, he decided to do the right thing and perform his nephew's duty.

*Besides*, thought Raul, *maybe that pretty nurse will be there.*

Sure enough, she was. Kara opened the door.

"Hello!" Raul said, way too eager, feeling like a teenage boy talking to the hot girl two grades above him.

"Hi Mr. Salazar," she said, flashing her pretty smile. "Was Ramon expecting you? He did not mention it."

"No. I thought I would pay him a surprise visit. Is it a bad time?"

"Not at all. I am sure he will be delighted. Please, come in."

"How's the old man been treating you?" said Raul after making his way inside.

"Good. He…is never mean," she said.

Raul laughed.

"A strong endorsement," he said sarcastically.

"He is a good man, I think. He is just… a little inappropriate sometimes."

"I see. Would you like me to talk to him for you?"

"No please. It is fine."

"It would be no problem."

"No, I don't want to make an issue."

"Understood." Raul put his palms out – the universal sign for surrendering the issue.

He began to make his way upstairs when he turned around.

"Kara?"

"Yes?"

"You know the only reason he acts that way is that he doesn't get to spend much time around pretty girls these days."

Raul felt a little nervous about his fairly direct attempt at flirtation. He wondered if it made him no better than his uncle. Nevertheless, he couldn't help himself. He didn't spend much time around pretty girls these days either.

Kara said nothing. She seemed to be digesting his comment in some deep place. His nerves increased and he felt the immediate need to say something further.

"You see," he said, "he's kind of like an animal kept in captivity, finally released into the wild."

"So I'm *the wild* in this situation? Like the outside?"

"I don't mean that you're wild…what I mean is…" *Say something smart, say something better*, he thought. "It's like when you're starving and somebody puts a big plate of food in front of you…"

Kara's eyebrows arched, curious to see where this was going.

Raul laughed. *Well that couldn't have gone any worse so quickly.*

"I guess I just wanted an excuse to say that you were pretty," he admitted. "Sorry if that makes me no better than the old man."

"It's okay," she said. "Thank you for the compliment."

"Alright, and now I will go upstairs for real."

Raul visited with his uncle for about an hour. They talked about news and stocks and sports. Basically they created their own conversational version of the newspaper. Raul kept up the conversation serviceably, which was an impressive feat considering he spent the entire time thinking about Kara.

He felt foolish. There was no way a young girl like that would be interested in him. It had just been so long since he had even thought about the possibility of romance that the wildfire in his mind spread a bit out of his control following the initial spark.

When he eventually descended back downstairs he was almost afraid to see her.

Kara, however, seemed perfectly receptive to his presence.

"Good time?" she asked.

"Spectacular," he said. "How was your time?"

"My time?"

"You know, hanging out down here?"

She laughed. "My time was very good. Thank you for asking."

"You are very welcome."

"Can I make you some lunch? You said before you were starving?"

"No, that was just…"

Kara smiled, indicating that she was joking.

"Oh, I gotcha," he said.

She laughed.

"Still, I am a little hungry," he admitted.

"I only have food here right now. Not women. Is that okay?"

*This girl has some spunk*, he thought.

"Yes, food will be fine."

He sat at the kitchen table as she made lunch for both of them and Raul's awkwardness gracefully settled down. He asked Kara about her life. She told him about her childhood in Tijuana. He told her about trips he had taken to Mexico. They discovered they were familiar with some of the same restaurants and gushed over impeccable food for several minutes.

"We should stop talking about this," she said eventually.

"Why?" he asked.

"You will not enjoy what I am making at all if you are thinking about the meals back home."

He laughed.

When she sat down at the table with the plates, Raul spotted something which nearly destroyed his hunger: A wedding ring on Kara's finger.

He forced a first bite of the sandwich she had given him down his throat. He partly wanted to make an excuse to leave right then, but he wished to be polite. He internally told his unreasonable hopes to take the rest of the day off.

"I didn't know you were married," he said.

She looked at her ring. She went silent for a moment. She seemed confused in some way.

"I..., I'm not married," she said. "I just wear this to keep men from hitting on me."

She was blushing intensely. He supposed she was embarrassed to admit this. He also thought it was interesting that she revealed the full truth to him instead of just vocally furthering the lie that was already displayed on her hand.

"Understood," he said. "Most men don't know how to treat a lady."

"Most men, but not all?"

"Not all."


Kara wasn't sure why she told Raul that she wasn't married. The words escaped her mouth before she questioned the emotions that persuaded her to say them.

For a moment, after Raul left, she tried to justify her mistruth by thinking that it wasn't *really* a lie since she wasn't *really* married. Dan had asked her to fake marry him. Their union was just a fiction being used to fool the government. He had made that abundantly clear.

But then she realized she could have just as easily told Raul the full scope of the situation. Instead, she had untruthfully claimed that she wore the ring to scare men away. There were only two conclusions that could be drawn from how she had acted. One: She didn't want Raul to know she was in a romantic relationship. Two: By "admitting" to him that she wore the ring to scare off men, she was (by the logic of her lie), openly not trying to scare him off. She was actually inviting his pursuit.

*Do I want Raul to pursue me?* she questioned.

She genuinely was not sure.

The opening months of her marriage certainly had not been the romantic heaven she had always dreamed of.

As soon as they had returned to California from Hawaii, Dan had set the ground rules.

"We'll continue just like we have been," he said. "You'll stay in L.A. during the week and stay at my place on the weekends. We'll move some of your things to my place to make it look like we live together in case the USCIS officials stop by. And I'll give you a couple pairs of my clothes to leave at your apartment just in case they drop by there. We can say we're keeping your apartment while you try to find a new job in San Diego."

"Okay," she said, not just then, but whenever Dan doled out instructions. He had the whole thing worked out in his head and he didn't seem to feel the need to consult her opinion.

Kara felt both insulted by this and, in direct contradiction, also relieved. Part of her wished she had more direct say as to the nature of their "marriage." She would have liked to see Dan more. If he had asked, she might have been fine with the idea of *actually* looking for a job in San Diego and living with him full time.

However, she was also glad he was so confident. She had been extremely nervous about her green card interview at the U.S. Citizenship & Immigration Services building. It soothed her nerves a great deal how Dan took charge of their deception. She didn't have to do any planning. She just had to do exactly as Dan told her.

The interview had taken place two months earlier. As Dan's car got nearer and nearer to the office, Kara's stomach twisted up with nerves until a near tornado of panic threatened to suck her in whole.

Not wanting to embarrass herself in front of her cool, calm, and collected man, she tried to keep her mouth shut and her concerns unvoiced. But when Dan's GPS informed them they were only one mile from the destination, the pressure proved too much and her worries came out firing like an air force assault of anxiety bombs.

"What if they don't believe us—what if they don't believe me—oh Dan, this is wrong—will they know?—can they tell—what if they know— ." And so on.

"Woah," said Dan. He pulled over to the side of the road. "Take a deep breath, Lovey."

Kara did as he asked. The infusion of air into her lungs didn't particularly help soothe her.

Dan took her hand. "There is nothing to worry about. I promise you. There is no reason for them not to believe us because the story we are about to tell them is true. We met. We fell in love. We got married."

*I just hate to lie*, she thought. Yet Dan truly did not seem to believe there was anything false about their marriage. (Even though he was the one who used the term "fake marry" when he proposed to her). It was all very perplexing and Kara needed her mind as sharp as possible. She could not be confused between what their marriage seemed to be and what they had to tell the officials their marriage was and whatever the hell Dan thought their marriage was. She needed to be poised and sure and have one story only.

Dan could still see the concern in her face. He looked right at her with the almost cocky level of confidence that won her over the first time she saw him.

"This is going to go great. I would never let anything bad happen to you."

Kara nodded her head and decided to believe him. She didn't have much other choice.

The local USCIS building was buzzing and bustling with folks of all shapes and sizes and races, speaking every manner of language, all blurred together into one booming sound of human communication in its loveliest and harshest varieties. As with most California immigration centers, those of Hispanic descent, like Kara, were the majority, but they were by no means the only ones hoping to gain citizenship in the good ol' U.S. of A.

She and Dan made their way slowly to the front desk, in line behind a shaking mother with a baby in each arm and a two year old gripping her right knee for dear life. Dan held her left hand with his right. In his other, he gripped their album of wedding photos – an essential piece of evidence for proving the validity of their union.

Once they finally got to speak with the clerk, they found out there was more waiting in store. They had to each fill out a pile of forms about as thick as the dictionary and were told their names would be called when someone was ready to see them. Once she finished with the documents, Kara felt momentarily relieved until she realized that at least the questionnaire had given her mind some distraction. Waiting without activity was incomparably worse and her heartbeat steadily increased its irksome thumping. Throughout Dan remained remarkably calm. A very small part of Kara felt pissed off by how little concern he showed since this was such an important, dramatic moment in her life. Mostly though, she was glad that her "husband" was a source of strength in this moment of stress. "He is my rock," was something she had heard American women say about their men. She now thought she understood the aphorism.

"Mr. and Mrs. McCoy?" she heard through the din of accents and inflections.

A hard bodied woman with an imposing clipboard had emerged from the uncomforting fluorescent back hallway. She was looking around the room for Kara and Dan.

Dan stood up immediately. A welcoming smile was plastered across his face. "We're right here," he said.

"I'm Agent Seckler," she said. She did not return Dan's smile. "Follow me."

They followed the agent to a plain, windowless backroom, shaped in a perfect square. The seating arrangement was laid out like a giant division symbol, with Agent Seckler on one side, Dan and Kara on the other, and a cold metal desk in the middle.

She spent several minutes poring over their forms. Kara found the wait excruciating. Dan seemed as relaxed as if he was spending a day on the beach.

Agent Seckler asked her first question while still looking at their forms.

"When was your first date?"

"May the 29th," Dan answered swiftly.

"Of this year?"

"Yep. 2013."

"That's an awfully short courtship, isn't it?"

"We fell in love really quickly."

"Kara, when did you know you were in love with Daniel?"

The sudden direct question took Kara by surprise and her skin prickled with worry. She remembered Dan's words. They were not lying. They really did fall in love. She just had to tell the truth.

"On the first date I thought I might love him. When we went to the taqueria at Venice Beach. I knew I loved him for sure when I woke up in his bed on our first weekend together."

Agent Seckler glanced up for the first time. She looked deep into Kara's eyes for a moment. Then she turned back to Dan.

The interview continued like that for what turned out to be only fifteen minutes, but which felt to Kara like at least an hour. Agent Seckler went back and forth from Dan to Kara asking them questions about each other – their personal lives, their knowledge of each other's jobs, their eating habits – testing out for any moment of hesitation or any tone of falseness in their stories.

Dan breezed through the proceedings, mixing lies seamlessly with the truth, giving no indication that there was any difference between the two. Kara felt as though even her completely truthful statements sounded less assured than Dan's false ones. Each time Agent Seckler's questions careened back in her direction she felt surprised and caught off guard. She didn't know what exactly the grading scale was for such a meeting but she was sure she was failing.

"Ms. Gomez, what is Mr. McCoy's phone number?" Agent Seckler asked after Dan had finished thoroughly detailing Kara's morning routine in response to a previous question.

This one took Kara by surprise. She always just selected Dan's name in her cell phone when she wanted to call him. This of course, was a perfectly reasonable response in the modern age, but in her panic, Kara foolishly pretended that the answer was just on the tip of her tongue.

"It's 858..." She was sure of the area code but not much else.

Agent Seckler stared her down with a rather judgmental curiosity. Dan looked utterly confused as to why she was answering the question. Kara almost made seven numbers up out of desperation before she remembered that Dan had written his number down on the forms sitting just across the desk and Agent Seckler would know she was wrong.

The silence continued on for a painfully long moment before Dan interrupted it.

"Do you know my phone number?" he asked casually. "I completely forgot yours once I programmed it in my cell phone."

"Well... I thought I remembered it," she said. "But I guess not."

Agent Seckler jotted something down on her notepad. Kara thought she was done for.

"May I see the wedding album?" she asked, when done writing.

"Of course," said Dan. He handed it over.

The agent spent a couple minutes flipping through the pages. Her expression betrayed no opinion at all.

"Where is this?"

"Hawaii," said Dan.

"Which island?" she asked. "Ms. Gomez?" she added before Dan had a chance to answer.

"It was Maui," Kara said, knowing the answer to that one, but still feeling dejected that she had already blown the interview. "It was lovely."

"Very nice," said Agent Seckler. "I was in Honolulu once. Beautiful place."

The agent's sudden conversational tone took both Dan and Kara by surprise. They sat up straight, both feeling that some crucial point of the conversation had been reached.

"Okay. I'm going to ask that we hold on to this wedding album while we go over everything, the license, marriage certificate, etc.," said Agent Seckler. "You'll get it back when we approve your application."

*When* we approve your application. Dan and Kara each took special notice of that crucial word usage.

"Mr. McCoy, you are not just entering into this marriage with Ms. Gomez so that she can obtain her green card and ultimately her American citizenship are you?"

"No, not at all," said Dan.

"You are aware that if you are lying to me and subverting the marital pathway to citizenship, and the lie is discovered, that you can be fined up to two hundred and fifty thousand dollars and face up to five years in prison?"

"I am."

Agent Seckler smiled. It was the first time during the entire interview she had looked even mildly pleasant.

"Okay, well we're good for now. You will get a notification of our decision in four to six weeks. I wouldn't worry too much though."

Kara felt the most tremendous relief flush throughout her body. Dan took her hand. He smiled at her – that wonderful confident smile that confirmed everything was going to be alright.

"It's not a hundred percent, but I can almost always tell when two people really love each other," she said.

Kara had received her green card exactly four weeks later. In the meantime she kept Dan's condo fully stocked with her personal items. A USCIS representative could still stop by anytime, he said. Though he didn't seem to love the appearance of her tampons on the top of his toilet.

"Do you have to keep this here?" he asked.

"You said to make it look realistic," she replied.

Dan seemed to look for a counterargument but could find none.

Stray box of tampons on Dan's toilet aside, things pretty much went right back to the way they were before all of the dramatic marriage commotion. Just as Dan had wanted.

Kara worked for Ramon during the week and came down to see Dan on the weekends. Dan started traveling to New York more for his appearances on Financial Network. At first these trips were almost always during the week, but slowly Dan became unavailable on certain weekends as well.

Still, the time she did spend with Dan was as wonderful as ever. They laughed, they ate, they loved. They had everything but a future.

When she was with Dan, Kara felt like she never wanted to be anywhere else. When she was apart from him she felt a desperate longing for something more.

That night she returned home and thought about Raul and the lie she had spoken. Then she thought about Dan and the truths she had left unsaid. She cuddled up with Ricki.

"You're the only one I really have Ricki," she said.

Ricki licked her face.

"If only it were legal to marry dogs in this country," she said.

# 9

Raul was back at Ramon's the next day.

"Back so soon?" Kara asked, surprised and glad to see him. She did not analyze her reaction for fear of what it might imply.

"Yeah, I think I may have left something in my Uncle's room," he said unconvincingly.

"Oh. What?" she asked.

"My…It was my…" he paused, sighed, laughed. He looked at Kara like she was in on the joke but she had no idea what was going on.

"I suppose I should have thought that part out," he said.

Kara said nothing. She waited to see where this was going.

"I'm a terrible liar," he said, laughing again. "The truth is I came to see you."

"Me?"

"Yeah. I feel like I'm about to ask you to prom or something."

"Prom?"

"Look, Kara, I swear I never do this, but…would you be interested in going out sometime? I know you said you wear that ring to prevent men from asking you out, but then I thought that it must mean something that you told me that instead of saying you were married like you probably usually do. But maybe I was just reading too much into the whole thing. Actually, I'm going to stop talking now."

He was really nervous. It was readily apparent. Kara found it rather sweet. It was all so different from Dan, whose heart rate probably wouldn't rise if he were he on a faulty plane falling towards the earth at a violent speed.

It was a moment of truth for Kara. Dan had openly given her permission to go out with other men. She found Raul attractive but not in the all-powerful way she did Dan. He did seem genuinely kind, which was appealing, but then she barely knew him.

Yet still, she found herself wanting to say yes. Maybe it was just a bitter reaction in wanting to punish Dan for his inattentiveness. Females had a reputation for playing these sorts of games with men. It wasn't usually her style but at the moment she could see the appeal. She looked somewhat forward to telling her "husband," she would be going out with another man. Perhaps if he realized he was really under threat of losing her he would want to see her more.

Besides, Raul had worked up the courage to ask her out. She had told him she was single so saying no would seem like a rejection for no other reason than complete disinterest. She couldn't stand the idea of being so mean.

"Sure," she said. "When is good?"

"How's Saturday night?" he said.

She was supposed to go see Dan, of course. She didn't really want to cancel, but she said yes anyway.

"Great!" said Raul. "I'll pick you up at eight." He turned around and walked out. Thirty seconds later, he returned. "Where do you live?" he asked.

Dan was in his bedroom, repacking the suitcase he had just emptied when the phone rang. It was Kara. He was planning on calling her very shortly. Jim Roberts had asked him to come out to New York again that weekend. He did feel a little bad because he had just been there the previous weekend and the trip would result in him and Kara being apart for the longest time since they had started dating, but he could hardly say no. He heard the rumbling. There was a chance he was going to be offered his own show. The opportunity of a lifetime. He was sure Kara would understand. She was so reasonable. That was one of the things he loved about her.

He answered the phone.

"Hey Lovey," he said.

"Hi."

"What's up? How's your week going?"

"It's fine. Listen, so I was calling because I cannot make it down this weekend."

Dan was surprised but he didn't think much of it. Mostly, he was relieved because he wouldn't let her down for not being around himself.

"Oh, don't worry about it," he said. "I actually have to go to New York."

"Really? Again?" she said. She sounded annoyed, which Dan thought odd, since she apparently wasn't available anyway.

Dan did his best not to let it bother him. Kara wasn't typically one to start irrational arguments.

"Yeah, Jim wants me to come out to do a couple more spots," he said. "Things are going really well. I've got a good feeling something big might be coming soon."

"Oh. That's really great," she said, though her tone didn't match her words. Dan thought he heard a sigh sneak through.

"Look," Dan said, trying to head off whatever conflict was forming before it started, "I know it's tough to go to this much time without seeing each other. I don't like it either."

"It's just that…"

Kara didn't finish her sentence so Dan felt the need to encourage her.

"Just that what?"

"Well I thought after we got…After I got my green card that we would see each other more. Instead it's been even less."

"I'm sorry. Look—" An idea suddenly struck him. He wasn't sure why it hadn't occurred to him before. "Why don't you come with me to New York this weekend? I'll be busy during the day but we could spend Saturday night together. And you've never seen New York. It's not at all like our California cities. It's definitely something you should see."

"Oh…I can't," she said.

"Oh c'mon, it'll be fun," he said, excited about the idea now that he had put it out there. He had already forgotten about her ambiguous other plans.

"I cannot," she said. "Because…I have a date."

There was a long silence. Dan tried to digest what he had just heard. He wanted to pretend it was a joke but he knew Kara's delightful humorous tone too well to think she was anything but completely serious.

"Hello? Daniel?" she said, unsure if they had lost their connection.

"Yes, I'm here," he said. "I'm sorry, the phone must have had some feedback. I thought you said you were going on a date." He was fully aware he had heard her perfectly clearly.

"I did. I am."

"Well…" Dan tried to think of what to say. He felt an itchy infusion of bitterness. "Well… I mean I guess we knew this day would come eventually. I didn't think it would be so soon but… I mean, if you think that this man can give you the life you want then I think you should give it a shot. I want the best for you."

"It's just a date," said Kara sheepishly. "You said I should—"

"I know. And I hope it goes well."

Silence.

"Well I have to finish packing for my plane," said Dan, "So I have to go. I'll talk to you later okay?"

"Okay," said Kara.

"Bye."

"Bye."

Kara hung up the phone. She felt awful. She was incredibly conflicted about turning Dan down on his offer to go to New York. She would have felt bad about canceling on Raul, but she was fairly sure that was not her main reasoning for saying no.

In truth, she wanted to feel in control of the relationship for once. Dan had dictated every term since the beginning and she was tired of it. She wanted to be a co-pilot, not a passenger. What was that thing he had said when she had first seen him speak with Ramon? *Only you can make your own decisions, be your own pilot.* Something like that. She wanted to take that advice. Not for stocks, but for her love life.

It was instinctual, turning him down. It felt like the right decision, even though it tore her up inside to make it.

*We'll probably be back together in San Diego next weekend and everything will be fine,* she thought. She figured she would forget all her twisted emotions when she saw him again. She would remember just how much she loved him.

Still, she wondered: *What if this is the beginning of the end?*

Raul took her to an authentic Mexican restaurant. His shared cultural heritage made his instincts for Kara's native food far stronger than Dan's. If she closed her eyes when she bit into the empanadas she briefly felt as if her soul had been sucked back into moments from her past, chatting with Teresa at a neighborhood eatery after school.

"Are you alright?" he asked, noticing the pain on her face.

Kara supposed it must be outwardly evident whenever she thought of Teresa – the pain of the loss was so all-consuming. Usually though, no one was around to look at her when she let the past enfold her in its bittersweet blanket.

"Just fine," she said. "This food reminds me of home."

"I'm sure it's not as good."

"It's terrific. The best I've had in the States."

"Good, I'm glad you're enjoying it," he said. "I was born here you know."

"At this restaurant?" she joked.

He laughed.

"No. Although that would explain my extra pounds."

Kara smiled. Enough to acknowledge his jest, but not too much to seem as if his weight were a detriment. She did not consider Raul fat. He was just *big*. Tall. Wide. The type of man who's body could provide shelter from a storm. He did not have Dan's matinee idol looks and figure, but he wore his large frame with comfort.

"I meant I was born in America," he said. "Here in Los Angeles. I just didn't want to act like I have a special ability to know Mexican food more than the locals. Only for you to later find out that I was a fraud the whole time."

"I do not think you are fraud."

"Good," he said.

Actually, she thought he was just about the most genuine man she had ever met. There was an impenetrable mystery about men like Dan that was undeniably appealing, even if it was frustrating in day to day interaction. Raul gave off a sense that his entire persona was right there for the plucking, if one only prodded gently. He had a sort of sturdy vulnerability. It didn't hit her with nearly the same guttural desire as Dan's curtain of emotion, but it was very likeable.

"Do you miss home?" he asked.

"Sometimes," she said. "I miss my family."

"Are you very close with them?"

"Yes, I love them a great deal. They are the main reason I am here."

"What do you mean?"

"My father, he is still working as a laborer – or he was. He got hurt. He is much too old for that kind of work. He needs to retire but they don't have the money. I have been sending some home each month."

"That's really noble of you."

"Not really. It's just the right thing. My mother and father gave me every-thing growing up. Food. Shelter. Love. This is my way to pay them back for what they gave me."

"Family is very important."

"You are very nice to visit your Uncle like you do."

Raul laughed. "Do you mean, because it's so much effort to be in the same room as him?"

Kara looked away briefly, then said with confidence, "No. That is not what I meant."

"I'm just kidding with you. I mean I know my Uncle can be an obnoxious old codger, and there are certainly times when I'm not in the right mood to spend time with him, but I still do love him. He helped me a great deal grow-ing up. I owe him for that. And he does have liveliness about him which is quite impressive in his old age. I only hope to have half that much spirit when my body starts to rebel against me."

She laughed. "Do you want a family of your own someday?" she asked.

"Another one?" he said casually.

"*Another* one?" she repeated back to him in a completely different tone, unsure what he meant.

"Well yeah. I have two children. Nick and Elizabeth, who we call Lizzie. They're eleven and seven." He saw that she was surprised. "I'm sorry. I guess I thought you knew. I figured Ramon talked about me. Very narcissistic I suppose."

"I thought you were not married?" she said, less accusatory than discouraged.

"*Oh*," he declared loudly, finally keying in to her thought process. "No. I'm not. I was. I've been going through a rather unpleasant divorce for the last year."

"I'm surprised," she said.

"What? That I'm divorced."

"Yes."

"Why?"

"You seem so nice."

"Even nice people get divorced."

"Yes. Of course. I didn't mean…I'm not sure what I meant."

"That wasn't the right response anyway. I'm sure my ex-wife would have a field day with me answering you that way. What I should have said is – I'm not always nice. But I'm glad that you think I am."

"I'm sorry to hear about your divorce. That must be hard."

"Thanks. It was. Really rough actually. But you know what? As painful as my marriage ending was…I got my kids out of it. And I would do anything for them. So I have no regrets."

Kara found the sentiment very beautiful. She was touched. She was also not just ready to let the conversation go. Whatever the nature of this date, or any other date she might go on, she didn't want to be caught by surprise again when it came to the crucial factor she needed in a mate.

"So would you ever consider having another child?"

She spotted a fleeting, but noticeable, wave of tension wash over his face. Then he clamped down and gave the question some serious thought before responding.

"Yes," he said. "Were it with the right person."

Kara had a good time with Raul. A really good time. A much better time than she had planned on having. A much better time than she had wanted to have.

By the time he took her back to her apartment building and walked her to her door, she was operating in two distinct, wildly contradictory modes.

The outward mode consisted of readily enjoying Raul's company and not hiding it. She laughed at his jokes. His witticisms were less sharp than Dan's – but his soft form of humor was not without its considerable charm. She felt great comfort in his open demeanor. He was someone with whom she felt she could be truly relaxed.

The inner mode consisted of alarm sounding, high threat level operations. *What the hell am I going to do if I start having feelings for Raul on top of my existing feelings for Dan?* Panic set in – her thoughts weaved and spiraled and tried to form a plan of attack before the situation had a chance to lock into its potentially tragic position.

"Thank you for a lovely evening," said Raul as they reached the front doors of her building.

"Thank you," said Kara, the words infused with a strong validity so he would know she meant them.

Raul took her hand and kissed it. It was a somewhat cheesy gesture, but Kara was pleased with his throwback gentlemanliness. She smiled brightly.

"May I see you again?" he asked.

"Hmm. I will think about it."

Raul looked discouraged.

"Okay. I thought about it. Yes, you may," Kara quickly added. The outward mode answered enthusiastically before the inner mode had a chance to voice its conflicted opinion.

Raul smiled. "I look forward to it," he said. "I'll call you soon. Goodnight Kara."

"Goodnight."

He walked off.


Jim Roberts and four other steel eyed network bigwigs were already seated around the dark wood conference table in hard leather chairs when Dan entered the room.

Dan wore his nicest suit. (Still no tie though – he had a severe mental allergy to ties. They were the noose that hung the masses who didn't bother to think for themselves. Or so he had thought up in one of his rare "poetic" moments.)

"Jim, good to see you again," he said, doling out as firm a handshake as he could muster.

"Dan, a pleasure as always," said Jim. "Have a seat."

Dan had expected to be introduced to and shake hands with the other senior executives, but apparently the expressionless old men watching him were mere statuesque observers, here to take stock of the situation silently before returning to their gold plated mansions.

"Dan we brought you in here today to discuss your ratings. They have not been what we expected."

Dan's optimism dissipated.

"No?"

"No," said Jim. He let a tense moment hang in the air. "They have been phenomenal."

Dan took a short breath of belief. He held his annoyance at Jim's unnecessary dramatics firmly inside.

"People are really connecting with you," Jim continued. "Your tracking is through the roof."

"That's great to hear," said Dan.

"For you and us both. You may remember when we first met we said we'd see how things went and then talk about you getting your own show."

"I might recall that."

"So you're interested?"

"Yeah, I think so," said Dan, feigning controlled enthusiasm.

"Glad to hear it. We're interested in signing you to a two year contract. We would start you out with a strong lead in and see where things go from there. Two months of preparation and a likely premiere in January. We'll have an official meeting with your lawyer to negotiate the specifics, including a nice salary for you, but those are the broad strokes. Are you interested?"

"Absolutely. I do want to say though – I want the same level of latitude I've had so far. I still want the freedom to speak off the cuff. I want to be honest.

And— "

"—and you don't want to wear a tie?"

Dan laughed. "Exactly."

"You really hate those ties."

"I really do."

"I'm sure we can put that in the contract. The only other thing is this. We would need you here in New York. Full time. I know there have been times we have had in you on via satellite but in order for you to have your own show we need you in our East Coast studio. Is that a problem for you?"

Dan hesitated for just a moment. His face remained blank. He was very good at not betraying his inner emotions to the outside world. The Financial Network executives would never know the firestorm of cogs turning wildly in his head during that three second lull.

"No," he said. "No problem at all."


Dan had done his best not think about Kara on the plane ride to New York and he resumed his effortful forgetfulness on the ride back.

The truth was, the news that Kara was going on a date with another man hurt. It hurt deeply. He got choked up just thinking about.

He also wasn't sure what the hell he could do about it.

Dan had told her himself to look for another man who could give her what she wanted. He meant it too. In the end, he knew that it would be the right thing. He didn't wish to deny her the future she wanted because of the present he wanted.

But he never expected her to take him up on it so damn soon. He didn't expect he would have to say goodbye to her after only five months together. He thought they would ride out this "marriage" for the three years it took her to become a citizen.

What hurt just as much as the fact that she was dating, was how casual she seemed to be about it. He had told her that if she fell in love with a man who would give her a family, she should take the opportunity. This, however, didn't sound like any life goal affirming connection. It was "just a date," she said. *Well then why even bother with it*, he had wanted to say. He felt angry and sad and this new offer from The Financial Network just contorted his emotions further.

He couldn't possibly turn down the offer, of course. Nor did he want to. It was a dream come true – having his own show. It was a culmination of everything he had worked so hard for in the last several years, building himself up from another puppet of corporate interests in an independent success story. It was a life changer. Far more important than another girl. Even one he had fallen in love with.

"Are you alright?"

Dan was shaken out of his haze by the passenger sitting next to him.

"Huh?" he said.

"You're crushing that bag of pretzels," said the man.

Dan looked in his hand. His fist was tightly grasped around an open bag of pretzels he had presumably received from a flight attendant, though he had no memory of it. Crumbs were spilling onto his legs.

"Fine. Just fine thanks."

He tucked the pretzel bag in the seat pocket in front of him and, embarrassed, turned his head towards the window.

His thoughts played on repeat for the remainder of the six hour flight. He was immensely glad when the plane hit the ground.

As he walked through the airport halls towards the exit, perhaps detoxed by some physical movement, he felt clearer.

*I'll call Kara when I get home*, he thought. *We'll talk this out.*

Yet when he entered his condo and took out his cell phone, he couldn't do it.

One of the things that Dan thought made him so good at his job was his ability to acknowledge realities. Where other people insisted on acting based on what they wanted to believe, Dan acted on what he knew to be true. He also didn't let himself be affected by what he might have thought before. Whereas it was a common mistake to hold on to a stock you once thought would be viable long after it becomes clear it is not, Dan ignored his past feelings in favor of the logic of the present. This was all immensely helpful in the world of money. It was also quite beneficial when it came to human relationships.

It didn't matter what he had wanted three months ago, or one month ago, or yesterday. What mattered was what made sense today. Right now.

If Kara had moved on there was nothing to be done about it. It was going to happen eventually. She would call him if she wanted to see him again. They would have to get together periodically to see her USCIS agent anyway. He would leave it up to her to get in touch.

In the meantime, he would move his life forward. Dan reminded himself that he had faced true loss. This was nothing. Barely a bump in the road.

He kept his phone out. He called Coady.

"Hey, Dan, how are you?" he said upon answering.

"Very well my friend. So listen. How would you like to move to New York?"

"Hell yeah!" said Greg, drunk on two beers, when the Guns N' Roses song he had personally selected on the jukebox started to play.

Dan met Coady and Greg at The Haddock, a local bar. Though nothing was signed, Jim Roberts had given his approval for Dan to have some of his own guys on the team for his future show. Greg swiftly decided that three of them needed to hit the town and celebrate.

"*Welcome to Jungle! We got fun n' games!*" Greg sang, repelling females like a particularly potent brand of bug spray.

Dan and Coady shook their heads and laughed.

"That guy cannot hold his alcohol," said Coady.

Dan nodded his head in pitiable agreement.

"Still, I'm excited too. This is big, Dan."

"I know."

"So why do you seem more like somebody died than that you just got an offer to host a national TV show?"

Dan looked up at him. His track record of hiding his emotions was taking some major hits today. He just shrugged, not wishing to make up some verbal explanation.

"Oh God," said Coady, suddenly worried. "Somebody didn't die, did they?"

"No," said Dan, reassuring him. "Nobody died."

"Well I'm always here if you need somebody to talk to," said Coady, making a stab at real friendship with his often hard to read boss.

"Thanks Coady. I'm alright though. Really. Great actually. This is a great day."

"It is," confirmed Coady. He was still suspicious about Dan's down demeanor, but he didn't press the issue. He gave up and joined his drunken mate. He threw his arm around Greg, who was now serenading an averse group of college girls with his Axl Rose impression.

"He's single ladies!" said Coady.

"Are they with you?" said a voice to Dan's left.

He turned his head. A very pretty woman stood next to him at the bar.

"Yep, those are my men," he said.

"They're quite…lively," she said.

He chuckled. "So they are."

"How come you're not over there singing with them? You look like you probably have a nice set of pipes."

"You can tell that?"

"It's one of my many talents."

"Well actually," said Dan. "I'm saving my voice for my American Idol audition."

"Oh yeah?"

"Yeah. I think I've got a real shot now that Simon's gone."

The woman leaned in closer to him.

"Buy me a drink?" she said.

Dan hesitated. He thought for a long moment about what he wished to do.

"Sorry," he finally said. "I'm married."

# 10

"How are things going with my nephew?"

Ramon looked like a mischievous little boy asking a question in class he knew would embarrass his teacher.

"Good. Very good I think," said Kara, blushing.

She was somewhat surprised it had taken Ramon so long to question her about her new relationship. But then she and Raul hadn't been in any rush to mention its existence to him. They had both shared an unspoken sense that the news might make Ramon jealous and uncomfortable. She supposed Raul must have finally broken and called his Uncle the night before. They had been dating for a month and a half now and Raul kept saying he needed to tell the old man. He had just been reluctant to follow through.

"He is treating you well?"

"Very well."

She felt a pleasant little emotional tickle inside, thinking about just how well she was being treated. Raul was a true gentleman. It was very hard to believe him when he said that he had frequently been horribly mean to his ex-wife.

"I'll let you talk to her," Raul had said. "She'll tell you all my worst qualities....Actually on second thought I'm not ever going to let you talk to her."

Kara had laughed. She supposed he was telling her the truth, but it was often so hard to grasp the full complicated picture of a person. The current impression of someone else often seemed so total and final, even if there were inevitable depths hiding well beneath the surface.

"He seems very happy," said Ramon.

Kara smiled.

"I'm glad you two are together," said Ramon, alleviating her fears of bitterness from her employer. "Raul has not had the easiest time this past year and I think you're doing him a world of good. And, if I might say so, I think it's good for you as well. You're so tense. You need a man to…*loosen you up*… if you know what I mean."

Kara rolled her eyes. She had done this so much during her time at Raul's house, that she knew his ceilings like the back of her hand.

"I'm happy for you two," he concluded, reigning in the vulgarity for a rare note of simplified pleasantness.

"Thank you Ramon," she said.

"And if things don't work out," he said, "I'll just have Raul stop coming by."

"What?" asked Kara, confused.

"I'll just go to his house and visit him there. I don't want any awkward scenes and I definitely don't want a different nurse."

Another eye roll. Another glance at the familiar ceilings. An extra bit of mortification in the rotation.

"Relax Kara! I'm sure it won't be necessary. I've got a good feeling about you two."

She had a good feeling too. And a bad feeling. And a joyous feeling. And a sickening feeling. All kinds of feelings really. Too many for one person to bear. She wished she could clear some of them out, as if her mind was an emotional vacuum cleaner that was stuffed with the dust of her many moods and would function with smooth precision once empty.

Her affection for Raul wasn't the bolt of lightning that her passion for Dan was. It was gradual. Softer. Admittedly, probably lighter. It was a long lazy ray of sunlight which woke her up from a relaxed sleep instead of a jolt of electricity blasting everything in sight to a blissful bright void. It was warm and comforting. It was a romance she could get a handle on, instead of one that could evaporate at any time.

She and Raul spent their time together in much the same way that she and Dan had. They went to restaurants. They went to the beach. They played with Ricki. (Raul was much more immediately taken with her then Dan had been, though, to his credit, Dan had become much more affectionate with Kara's constant companion over time). They even went salsa dancing on one occasion. (In this area, there was no comparison with Dan – Raul was an infinitely better dancer).

They had sex. Kara made Raul wait longer than she had Dan. A full month. Five dates. Her delay had more to do with her lingering feelings for Dan than anything else. She didn't tell Raul this, of course. The two men were both similar and different as lovers. They each had a very masculine "take charge," mentality, but, in keeping with the rest of their personalities, Raul was much more gentle and Dan was more aggressive. (Though they were each quite capable of the opposite, even if it wasn't their base technique.) She didn't necessarily prefer either. Both men were more than capable of bringing her pleasure – the wonderful destination that was more important than the roads taken to it.

She could not say with any conviction that her feelings for Dan were lessening or that she liked Raul more than him. So she mostly avoided thinking about it. She tried to judge Raul on his own, independent of any comparison. From this perspective, she felt increasingly attached to him.

As for the man who was still her legal husband, Kara had barely spoken to him since that first awkward phone call when she had told him she was going out with another man.

He had called her a couple of weeks after that initial exchange to see how things were going. When she saw his name on the phone she had initially expected him to ask her to come down for the weekend. She knew if he did, she wouldn't have been able to resist saying yes.

Instead he had just asked about Raul.

"How are you?"

"Good," she said. "You?"

"Good," he said.

It was the tensest exchange of bland greetings she had ever experienced.

"Guess what?" he said.

"What?"

"They're giving me my own show. The Financial Network. They want it to premiere in January."

"That's great news!"

"It really is," he said.

He did not sound the least bit excited.

"So…," he asked, "are you still dating that guy?"

"Yes," she admitted quietly.

"You like him?"

"I do," she said, figuring there was no point in lying.

"Cool," he said.

It was not a word she had ever heard Dan speak before.

They exchanged a few more pleasantries, neither of them sounding like they had any desire to continue speaking, and then they said goodbye. Dan unenthusiastically said, "Let's talk soon." They hadn't talked since.

Preparing for "The Dan McCoy Show" (as the network uncreatively decided to call it) provided a hefty distraction from the other worries in Dan's life. "A herculean task," was an expression Dan was fond of, but had never had a chance to use in earnest before now. Putting together a TV show was a herculean task. It was amazing that any show had ever made it on the air, let alone the fifty thousand shows currently airing on the five hundred channels available in most households.

One could really get caught up in the time siphoning minutia of every little detail. It's nine a.m. and somebody asks you about the color of a pillar residing well to the left of screen, which will only be spotted by the viewer during the rare use of camera three, and soon enough it's noon and everyone is taking a lunch break and the network executive in charge of approving set decisions still is unsure about the decision of "red."

There was all the hiring and interviews. The putting together of a statistics team and a copyrighting team and a lighting team and a tech team. Greg and Coady, of course, spearheaded the tech team, but the network insisted they be rounded out by a minimum of ten other experienced professionals. Not to mention the graphics department and the guest bookers and the cameramen and many more.

It was amazing, Dan thought, how many people were required to put together what was primarily a one man show of mostly unscripted commentary based on events that happened predominantly on the day the program aired.

Still, Dan's somewhat sarcastic opinion of the probable over planning aside, he was loving every minute of it. It was work. Good mind focusing work.

All the work hardly left him any time to think about Kara.

Hardly any. But some.

His mind stubbornly refused to let her go. He kept hoping she would call and say things had ended with the other man she had been seeing. He wanted her to call and say "screw the future, let's live for now." He was well aware of how unlikely that was to happen.

He kept listening to that first voice mail she had left him.

"Mr. McCoy, my name is Kara Gomez. We met at the hotel earlier today.

And I just wanted to say that I liked your talk. And I liked meeting you too. And I would like to get some more of your…money wisdom…so, if you like, please call me."

Dan was never one to live in the past and yet here he was, replaying that message over and over, trying to recapture that wonderful moment when that brief magnificent summer still lay ahead of him.

Now it was a week before Christmas. The show was pretty much ready to go except for some final preparation that would be done after the New Year.

Dan was on a plane, waiting to fly out to California, where he would see out the rest of the calendar year, when he was affected by the stupidest, schmaltziest of sights.

He got up to the go to the bathroom and on the way back he spotted a couple sitting a few rows in front of him. They were a white husband and a Hispanic wife. The wife leaned her head on her husband's shoulder with her eyes closed. He held her hand. They had a child. A little girl. She sat next to them.

As Dan passed the little girl smiled at him and waved.

It almost made him angry how cliché of a sight it was – a glimpse at the life that he could have had if he had handled things differently – and how immediately it affected his emotions as if it was some profound vision.

He hurried back to his seat, his heart racing. He asked himself: *Just what is it that I want?* It was so galling that such a simple, fundamental question could be so hard to get a handle on.

*What if I've been wrong? What if what I think I want isn't actually what I want?*

Dan had been so confident all these years that no relationship could last. The memories of love's transient nature were so vivid and the observations of the frustrating marriages of those around him so acute. He was so sure he had no desire for fatherhood, yet here he was, struck by the most intense sensation of longing after seeing a child who might look like the one he and Kara would have. His mind was not changed but a seed of doubt about his future desires was planted.

Did he real feel differently than he always had? Had his opinion on the matter really shifted? Or was he just so in love with Kara at the present moment that he was convincing himself to consider an irrational alternative for the sake of winning her back? He wasn't sure. But he knew he needed to see her. He needed to talk to her.

He called her as soon as he got off the plane. It went to voicemail.

"Hey Lovey. It's your husband. I was hoping we could together this weekend. I need to talk to you. Give me a call when you can."

Kara had just finished dinner with Raul when her phone rang.

They were at his apartment. He had made them quesadillas. Raul was a spectacular cook.

At the end of the meal, Raul had told her he had a special surprise. He had made her close her eyes. When she opened them a small velvet box containing a pair of beautiful sapphire earrings sat in front of her.

"Raul!" she said, not finding the words for any other reaction.

"Do you like them?" he asked.

"Of course! I love them!"

She picked up the box. Her eyes got lost in the glimmering light.

"Can you afford this though?" she said. "What with the divorce and your kids?"

"It's fine," he said, reassuring her. "Don't worry about money."

"Oh, Raul."

She threw her arms around him and kissed him.

"Try them on," he said.

That was when her phone rang. Kara's cell phone hardly ever went off so Raul, curious, couldn't help himself but have a peek at the name on the screen.

"Who's Dan?" he asked.

She immediately rejected the call. "My husband," she said carelessly, still wrapped up in the swirling pleasure of the gift.

Raul laughed.

"Very funny," he said.

Kara realized the depth of her mistake as soon at the words came out of her mouth. Raul could tell that there was something very wrong in her expression. She looked crestfallen and hopeless. Deep confusion clouded over him.

A terrible moment of silence passed between them. There was only truth in her eyes. He could see it.

"Kara," he said softly. "Do you *have* a husband? You said you wore that ring to deflect attention."

She fell into a chair. She searched frantically for a reasonable way to explain the situation. He waited patiently for an answer, which made it all the more difficult. He was not angry. Not yet. Just deeply, intensely, dejected.

"Okay…Raul…I'm sorry. I did get married— to a friend. He is just a friend. And he married me because my visa was going to expire and I was going to be deported."

"I don't understand Kara," he said, at once so distant from her.

She started to cry.

"I only did it so I could stay here and keep working so I could send money to my family."

"Who is this man?"

"Just a friend."

"How long have you been married to him?"

"It does not mean anything. I just did it for my green card."

Raul slammed his hand down on the table. His growing anger escaped him. Kara jumped back at the sound.

"Kara why didn't you tell me this in the first place? Why did you lie about stopping men from hitting on you?"

"Because… I thought that… I did not think you would be interested in someone who married for her citizenship."

"I don't give a shit about that! But this… You lied to me Kara!"

He got quiet for a moment. The wheels were turning in his head. When he spoke again he sounded much more civil, and much colder.

"I'm sorry but I don't know what to believe," he said. "I have to process this. You need to go."

"Raul, please," she said through tears.

"I have to think this through."

He turned his back to her.

She forced herself to stand up and gathered her coat. Before she left she took the one earing that had made it into her ear out and placed it back in the box with its partner.

"I'm sorry," she said again.

She made her way out the door, looking at Raul. He did not turn around.

"Hi," Kara said simply, when Dan answered the phone.

"Hey there."

"I got your message."

"Yeah. How are you?"

"Fine. You said you want to get together? Should I come down to you?"

"No. No that's okay, I'll come up to LA. When's convenient?"

"Anytime. Saturday."

"Okay. Okay sounds great, I'll come up then."

It was strange for Kara to invite Dan into her apartment. He had never been inside before.

"This place is nice," he said. He sounded genuine, but surely he was just being polite.

"It's small," she said.

Small was her apartment's defining characteristic. It didn't have enough space to make room for any other attributes.

He gave her a big hug. She returned in full, glad to feel his strong arms around her.

"Can I get you something?" she asked.

"Glass of milk?"

"Really?"

"No I'm just kidding. Who drinks milk?" he said, with a smirk.

"Very funny."

"Actually, you know I wouldn't mind some milk though."

"Really?"

"No, I'm still kidding."

She laughed and slapped him on the arm.

"Sorry," he said. "Can we sit down?"

"Sure."

They sat on the couch. Ricki immediately lodged herself between them. She used her arms to perch herself up on Dan's leg and lick his face. He was surprisingly agreeable to Ricki using her tongue like it was a mop and his face was a cafeteria floor. Kara had to force her down.

"Okay, girl. Let the man breathe."

"Thanks," he said.

"So how are you?"

"I'm fine," he said. "I'm happy to see you."

"I'm happy to see you too."

"I'm sorry we haven't talked at all lately."

"Yeah…" she said. Not sure exactly how to broach the subject of *why* that had not spoken.

"Look," he said, "There's something I want to say."

"Okay." Kara felt suddenly very nervous, though she was unsure what she feared.

"So I told you that I'm going to have my own show on the Financial

Network."

"Yes. That's great! I am very happy for you."

"Thanks. We're premiering in January. Just after New Years."

"Soon."

"Right. Soon. And the thing about it is, I have to move to New York."

"Oh."

"They're based there and flying back and forth or doing it remotely won't work. I've already got a place. I'm going to rent out my condo in San Diego for the time being. I don't want to sell it in case the show doesn't work out. I sure will miss living there."

Kara nodded. She wasn't sure what to say. She supposed this was the official goodbye. She had commenced their separation when she had started dating another man and now Dan was finishing it with his departure across the country.

"So the thing about it is, I haven't liked being apart from you. I know you've been seeing this other guy but... I want you to come with me."

"Come with you?"

"To New York. I want you to move with me to my new apartment in New York. If you'd like to."

Surprise descended on Kara like nausea. Pleasure and terror and shock all mixed into one indigestible cocktail.

She stood up. She took a lap around the room.

"I looked into it," he said, "And I can get you a job with an agency like the one you have now. You can bring Ricki and she can keep you company while I'm working. Kara. I don't want to lose you."

He gave her a minute to digest the information. She continued to pace. Ricki barked, concerned that something was amiss.

Kara made herself stand still. She closed her eyes, took a deep breath, then looked right at Dan.

"Are you saying you want to make our fake marriage real?" she asked.

"I don't honestly know Lovey. I just want you by my side."

"Well have you changed your mind about having children?"

Dan looked uneasy. He was tempted to tell her what she wanted to hear but he wanted to be honest.

"I don't want children now. I don't want to lie to you or lead you on. But I can't one hundred percent say what I'll want in the future. I'm not sure. But we could just live for now and see what happens then."

Dan's non-committal nature at this moment made her angry in a way that it never had before. She felt like she was coming apart at the seams.

"Do you still want to get a divorce in two and half years?" she said, exasperated. "Do you still want me to look for another man who can give me what I want?"

Dan had never really seen Kara get mad. It was off-putting. His conviction started to falter. He could see his plan falling to pieces in front of his eyes. The last thing he wanted to do was upset her. He wanted to make her happy.

"I don't know," he said. "We can do whatever you want. *You* can do whatever you want. If it didn't work out you can always come back to California. Look, I know I'm dropping a lot on you. Maybe I'm not being fair. But I wouldn't have been able to live with myself if I didn't take some action here."

Kara saw the pain in his eyes and calmed down somewhat. He was not trying to frustrate her. She knew that. She just wished he knew what he wanted. She wished the whole thing wasn't so damn complicated. But then, she supposed, real love was never simple. And dreams never had proper endings. You always woke up in the middle.

She sat down next to him and put her hand on his.

"This is a lot to think about my love," she said. "I did not expect this."

Dan looked away from her. "Is it that guy?" he asked. "Is he the reason you would hesitate to come with me?"

"Honestly," she said, "things are not great with him right now."

Dan looked back at her. A subtle beacon of hope seemed to flash across the dark islands of his eyes. He held back, not wanting to appear too excited. He took advantage of a nice new silence (Ricki's barking had ceased, apparently appeased that no danger was in sight) to try to think of the best thing to say.

"Look, I can't say for sure if I'll ever want... a family. All of that. But... maybe we could do something. Work something out. I don't know. Maybe."

As a well-spoken man of radio and television, Dan was ashamed by the jumble of words that had just tumbled out of his mouth. He also couldn't think of anything better to say. His long planted certainty against marriage and children were at war with his desire to sacrifice for Kara so he could be with her. He had way too much integrity to make a promise he wasn't sure he could keep, although he was tempted.

"Maybe," she repeated back to him, somewhat wanting him to feel the distaste of the word. She sighed. "I have to think this over Daniel," she said.

"I understand," he said.

They sat together, not speaking, not looking at each other, for a moment. Ricki looked imploringly back and forth at both of them, her tail wagging. She seemed to approve the idea of the gang getting back together even if her mother was unsure.

"I should go," Dan said.

He leaned over and kissed Kara lightly, lovingly.

Then he went.


Kara headed home to Tijuana almost immediately.

She didn't even think about it. It was completely instinctual. Her world was out of balance and she needed the solid foundation of family. Her family was really all she had, she realized, feeling terribly, unpleasantly fragile.

As she watched the California landscape fly by on the bus to the border, she thought of all of the people she saw all the time with their large groups of friends. She wondered what it would be like to have such a base of non-familial support. Teresa had really been the only close friend she ever had. She had been friendly with other girls over the years but none of those relationships had ever sparked enough connection to inflame something sustainable. Kara had always been the type of person who preferred the idea of one really close relationship to many minor ones. She was a classic introvert in this respect.

She supposed this was why the idea of finding a man was so important to her. She had always felt like one really strong connection could transcend everything else. She also felt that family was more important than friendship, because, one strong friendship aside, her own family was where she had always found meaning.

In this particular moment of hounding uncertainty, she wanted the comfort and strength of her father. But she knew she couldn't tell her parents the truth. The shame of having lied would be overwhelming.

So she went to see Carmen.

"Kara," her sister said with great shock when she opened the door.

"Hi," said Kara. She sounded breakable. Carmen could tell right away something was wrong.

"Come in! Come in! What a nice surprise!"

As soon as she walked in, Kara spotted Isabella, now over a year old, standing on her own two feet, looking curiously at the door to see who might be entering her home.

"Look who's here," Carmen said to her daughter. "It's your aunt Kara."

"Hi," said Kara to her adorable niece.

Isabella just stared up at her.

"Say hola," said Carmen.

"Hola," she said, sweetly, not fully pronouncing the L.

Kara smiled intensely. The smile almost induced tears. The preciousness of a child was almost too much for her to take at the current moment.

"She's perfect," said Kara.

"Eh. She's alright. She doesn't know how to poop in the toilet yet," said

Carmen.

Kara laughed.

"I love you sister," she said.

"I love you too," said Carmen. "Now sit down and tell me what's wrong."

Jorge was at work and Carlos was at school, so the sisters had plenty of time to talk without distraction, other than the occasional, mostly indecipherable inquiry from sweet little Isabelle.

Kara told Carmen everything. She told her about Dan's proposal of a "fake marriage," so that she could stay in the country and he could remain uncommitted. She told her about his declaration that she should look for another man who could give her a family if she wanted to. She told her about Raul and her unexpected, ever-growing feelings for him. She told about her lie to Raul about her marriage and how upset he was when he found out. And she told her about Dan's latest offer to move with him to New York.

Carmen, to her great credit, sat and just listened without feeling the need to interject jokes or judgment. She knew that Kara needed to express herself and she gave her sister what she needed.

For Kara, it was an unspeakable relief to let out all of the rumbling incidences and feelings in her head. It had not occurred to her all this time to really accept Carmen's offer of being someone she could talk to. She was extremely glad that she finally did.

"So what do you think?" said Kara, when she was all done telling her tale.

"I'm really not sure Kara. It is complicated, this life. Sometimes there is no right decision. You just have to do what feels right."

It was an answer filled with as much uncertainty as Kara already felt. Yet it was still a great comfort to share the uncertainty with someone else. She no longer felt as if she had to bear the burden alone. And that alone was touching in the deepest way.

"Thanks so much for listening."

"Of course. I'm your sister."

Kara threw her arms around Carmen and hugged her tightly. Carmen responded in kind.

"You should stay here for a couple of days. Christmas is Wednesday. You can spend Christmas with all of us. You obviously don't need to spend it with your husband like you originally said."

"I'm supposed to work on Monday."

"Call out sick."

"They say I am not allowed to call out right before a holiday."

"Who cares about them? You say this Ramon adores you. He won't let you get fired."

"What will we tell mama and papa?"

"That Dan had to go to New York. Or he had a family emergency. It doesn't matter."

"I don't like to lie to them."

"It's a little late for that."

Kara thought it over. All of Carmen's points were reasonable. And it would be lovely to spend Christmas with her family as she had always done.

"Okay," she said.

It all went as Carmen said. Calling out of work was not an issue. Her family did not question her fib about Dan spending Christmas in New York to prepare for his new TV show. (Though they did think it was quite horrible that the network would make him work over Christmas). And Kara was delighted to spend the holiday with her family.

While she was there, she was able to put all of her other worries and concerns by the wayside. She knew she would have to confront them again soon enough, but it was wonderful to find an oasis of effortless familial love in their midst.

Christmas was a day long celebration. They went to church in the morning and the rest of the day the Gomez household was packed with relatives.

As always, the house never seemed more natural than when it was filled to the brim with human beings.

Maria's home cooked meal was absolutely excellent. It was truly amazing the way her mother could feed so many people without any difficulty and nary a complaint.

"I love you mama," she told her.

"I love you too my girl," said Maria.

After dinner, Adriana, Martha, and some of the other cousins started a dance party in the backyard (as they were prone to do on every possible occasion), but Kara passed on the fun to sit on the couch and lean her head on the shoulder of her still recovering father.

"I love you papa," she told him.

"I love *you*," he said, as if it was the world's most affectionate competition.

Late that night, as the guests departed and Kara doled out one goodbye hug after another, Kara received a phone call.

Her heart pounded. She expected it to be Dan.

It was Raul.

She snuck into her room, closed the door, and answered.

"Merry Christmas," he said.

"Merry Christmas."

"I'm sorry to call you this late. Are you sleeping?"

"No. It's fine. I'm at home. I was just saying goodbye to some of my relatives."

"You're in Tijuana?"

"Yes."

"Oh. That's good."

"Yes, it is nice to be here."

Raul went quiet on his end. She could hear his breathing. She was not sure what to say so she just waited.

"I was feeling lonely tonight. My kids are with their mother and...I was wishing I was with you."

"Oh."

"I want to be with you Kara. Do you want to be with me?"

"Yes," she said. It was a truthful answer. The fact that she also wanted to be with someone else did not make it any less true.

"I'm glad to hear that. Look, I just need to ask you something one more time and then I promise I will never ask it again. I just want the truth. The full truth whatever it is"

"Okay."

"Is there anything serious about your marriage to this man?"

"No."

She lied immediately and instinctively, knowing any hesitation might give her away. She hated the fact that she was still lying but later she thought: complete honesty with someone you are in a relationship with was never really possible. There were too many precarious feelings involved. She also figured the fact that she lied to Raul so automatically must mean that she did not want to lose him. Deep down, she wanted to protect what they had and what they might have in the future.

"Do you love this man?"

"He is just my friend," she said. "I love him but not in the same way I love you. He is helping me and I care for him but it is not the same."

*God forgive me my lies,* she thought. Though as she spoke, she could feel herself letting go of Dan for good. The door was closing on their relationship once and for all.

"Then it does not matter to me," he said. "I want to be with you."

"Raul," she said, after a pause, "Do you think you could ever want another family? Could you ever want another family with *me*?"

Raul paused.

"The truth is Kara, the idea of getting married again and having more kids terrifies me... That being said, I feel strongly you can only ever make decisions in life based on how you feel now and just hope for the best later. So yes Kara, I do think I could have a family with you. In fact, right now, having a family someday with you is all that I want."

Dan was just returning from the beach when he found Kara at his condo, sitting on his doorstep.

"Hi" she said.

Dan knew right away that it was all over. Kara had a mournfulness about her that was unmistakable. This was an ending. This was a goodbye.

"Hi," he said. He sat down next to her.

Neither of them asked to go inside. It seemed somehow more proper to have the conversation outside. Perhaps neither of them wanted to cross through the proverbial "marriage threshold" of the doorway if their marriage was coming to a close.

"You're not coming with me to New York, are you?" he said.

"No. I can't," she said. She truly sounded sorry about it. "I'm going to stay with Raul."

"The other guy?"

"Yes."

"So things are going well with him again?"

She nodded. He digested the information.

"You really think he's the one?"

She became thoughtful.

"I think he is," she said.

Dan looked away from her. "Then if you're happy…I'm happy." He looked back. "I want you to be happy Kara. You know that right?"

"Of course."

They were quiet.

"I can't believe it's only been seven months since we met," he said. "It feels like so much longer. I mean it feels like it went by fast, but it also feels like it lasted a lifetime. I don't know if that makes any sense."

"It does."

They looked at each other without saying anything. It was like they were both running through all their memories of one another, attempting to store them for permanent recall.

"When do you leave for New York?" she asked.

"The thirtieth."

"Well you must make sure to bring plenty of warm clothes to bundle up. It is cold out there!"

Dan laughed.

"I'll be sure to do that."

"And we must keep in touch! I do not want to stop talking because of this. I want you to be my friend."

"Friend, huh?" he said. He considered the proposition. It didn't sound so bad. "Okay. I think I can do that."

"Good."

"I'm sorry I couldn't give you everything you wanted," he said. He was very sorry. But he also felt, saying it, once and for all, that he really never would have been able to give her what she wanted. He was fooling himself into thinking it was a possibility so that he could stay with her. He wished he could have had longer with her, but at least this way he would never disappoint her.

"You have given me so much," she said. "You have made everything possible for me. I can never thank you enough for what you have given me."

"I'll miss you," he said.

"I will miss you too," she said.

She leaned her head on his shoulder. He took her hand.

"We should gather up your stuff," he said.

"Yes. We should," she said.

Neither of them moved.

They sat like that for a very long time. They watched the sun disappear beyond the horizon and the day turn into night.

# 11

It was five minutes to midnight on New Year's Eve and Kara suddenly felt an incredible surge of happiness.

She was with Raul and his daughter Lizzie. She had been a little shy at first when they had picked her up, but she was sweet as can be and she seemed to warm to Kara as the hours progressed. Raul's son Nick was spending the night at a friend's house. Kara expressed regret that she couldn't spend the holiday with both of his children but Raul warned that Nick would not be nearly as friendly as his daughter when they did eventually meet. Kara said she was sure he was exaggerating, but Raul insisted.

"He'll probably see you as a threat and I apologize in advance."

"No apologies necessary. He is your son."

Raul had done a lot of apologizing for things that didn't happen yet in the past week. He apologized for when he would inevitably annoy her. He apologized for any time he might let her down.

His son wasn't the only one damaged by the divorce, Kara could tell. He was clearly trying to avoid whatever mistakes he felt he made last time. She thought all of his advance apologies were unnecessary. "Let us wait until you actually do something," she said. Nevertheless, she enjoyed hearing the apologies because they were Raul's way of committing to her for the long term. He wanted them to stay together well into the future, she could tell, and it was tremendously pleasing.

It had not been very long, yet Raul already felt like family. That was why she chose him, she supposed, beyond his willingness to eventually give Kara the future she wanted in a way Dan never would. It was his force of comfort. He was tremendously comforting. Kara felt she could wrap herself in his arms and withstand a long hard winter. Not that she would have to face such conditions in Los Angeles.

"Do it again Kara!" said Lizzie, excitedly.

Raul had just given them the paper noisemakers that unroll when blown into. He had said they were not to be used until midnight but the females in the room had impatiently overruled him and used theirs right away.

Kara playfully used her noisemaker like a sword to attack Lizzie's when it unfurled. Lizzie thought this surprise strike was just about the funniest thing that had ever happened. She insisted that they repeat their battle until their lungs ran dry.

"It's my own fault," said Raul, putting his fingers in his ears.

Kara leaned over to Lizzie and whispered something in her ears. The child laughed enthusiastically.

"On three," said Kara. "One, two, three!"

They both jumped on top of Ramon and attacked Ramon with the extended paper tubes of their noisemakers.

Lizzie fell to the floor, dying of laughter. She could not take the joy.

"Sorry my love," said Kara. She kissed Raul on the spots on his face where he had been hit. "All better?"

"Completely," he said. "Well maybe one more." He pulled her in and kissed her on the lips.

"Ooooh," said Lizzie, as any self-respecting six year old girl would.

This is happiness, thought Kara.

It had been such a crazy year. So much stress. So much joy. It was the most eventful and unpredictable year in her life. Dan had been such a huge part of it and she would not have traded the time with him for anything. But being here with Raul and Lizzie – it felt good. It felt right.

"The countdown's starting!" Lizzie screeched. "Ten! Nine! Eight!"

Raul and Kara joined in.

"Seven! Six! Five! Four! Three! Two! One! Happy New Year!"

Raul kissed Kara. Then he grabbed Lizzie and stuffed her in the middle of a big group hug.

*Yes*, Kara thought, *this is what I want.*


Dan opened up his calendar book and once again found himself looking at the page for January 10th.

*Has it been a year already?,* he thought.

He sat down at the incredibly comfortable Aeron chair that The Financial Network had provided for his office and looked out his window at his beautiful view of the Manhattan skyline.

The past couple of years he had begun thinking about this date days in advance, dreading his indecision and inevitable inaction. This year, however, he had been so busy with the show and so emotionally consumed with letting go of Kara that Sue's birthday had not occurred to him.

The first week of The Dan McCoy Show had gone off without a major hitch. The first week's ratings were respectable enough. Not numbers that would send the advertisers into a bidding war admittedly, but these things took time, or so Jim Roberts said.

"The network is *very* happy with the numbers," Jim assured him and Dan took his word for it.

The reviews were quite kind, which was encouraging. One (apparently influential) blogger had called Dan "a breath of fresh air in the increasingly hard to stomach world of poorly disguised corporate interest puppetry."

From a personal perspective Dan was rather enjoying being on the air. He always found a thrill in confidently delivering his expertise to a large crowd.

This was the largest crowd he had ever spoken to – even if they watched from the other end of a thousand tubes and wires.

The show was extraordinarily time consuming. More so than the planning stage ever prepared him for. He was not complaining. Work was just what he wanted right now and lots of it. It distracted him from thoughts about Kara. Somewhat anyway. She held a bit of a current monopoly on his consciousness.

Dan could not decide if he had any regrets. At least as far as his relationship with Kara was concerned. In order to have regrets, one must pinpoint a moment where you would have acted differently. Dan wished he could have had more time with Kara. He wished their relationship had gone better than it did. But he couldn't seem to pinpoint any moment in which he acted in a way that wasn't true to himself.

Sometimes, he figured, circumstances just don't go the way you want. There was nothing to be done about it.

One area where he was suddenly certain he *did* have regrets was with his relationship with his sister. Maybe it was his current loneliness influencing him, but he felt suddenly ashamed that he had gone this long without contacting the only family he had left.

He took out his cell phone and dialed Sue's number.

The phone rang several times. He figured she was not going to pick up, seeing his name on the screen.

Then she did.

"Hello," the voice on the other end said. There was a bit of a question mark in the greeting.

"Sue. Hi, it's your brother."

"Hi Dan," she said. It was clear she was not sure what to say.

"Sue…" He didn't know where to begin. He thought over everything he could say. He could apologize for the tremendously long time they had gone without talking. He could tell her that he hoped deeply the separation between them would end and that they could be family again. There was so much that could be said. So much that needed to be said. For starters, though, he would keep it simple.

"Happy birthday sis," he said.

# 12
## September 17, 2016

The room was filled with well-earned pride. It felt to Dan like a graduation day for adults, without the silly robes and hats.

Dan sat in a folding chair, next to the Salazars, Raul and Ramon, as well as Kara's many family members who had come up for the occasion. The university gymnasium that had been rented for the ceremony was filled with beaming parents and relatives and friends, all overcome with joy at the accomplishment of their loved ones.

*It's enough to make you feel guilty for having born here*, thought Dan, who had obtained his own citizenship simply by his mother giving birth to him in an American hospital.

Kara and the nineteen other inductees to the nation's exclusive club of human beings sat at the front of the room. They each waited for their name to be called by the USCIS speaker so they could receive their own certificate of naturalization.

"She's next," Raul said excitedly to Dan when the man sitting next to Kara was called to the podium.

Raul was rather fond of Dan. Kara warned Dan before the first time they had met that she had never told Raul the full truth of their relationship. She pleaded Dan to pretend they had merely been friends. Dan played his part well and Raul told him how "immensely thankful" he was for what he had done for Kara. He said Dan was a "hero."

Initially, Dan hoped to avoid meeting Kara's new love all together. But Kara insisted her story wouldn't make sense if her "friend" was so reluctant to meet her "boyfriend." She had begged him. Dan was a strong willed human in a lot of ways, but he was helpless to deny Kara something she asked for so directly. For all that had passed, he still loved her. He figured he always would.

So they had met and Raul had heaped Dan with praise he didn't deserve and Dan, much to his annoyance, found that Raul's immediate affection for him was mutual. Maybe it was the man's somewhat oblivious complete lack of suspicion or jealousy, but Dan thought Kara's soon to be second husband was very likeable. More importantly, he could see how happy Raul made Kara. And anyone that made Kara that happy was alright in his book.

"Kara Maria Gomez," said the speaker.

Kara's contingent in the gym went wild. Whoops and cheers and whistles. Dan clapped along admirably, unable to match the display of the Gomez clan, but happy to be part of their celebration.

Kara walked up to the podium and accepted her certificate. She smiled wide. It had been a long road, but she was finally here.

She did not accept her citizenship alone. Inside her was an ever growing life. She clutched her certificate in one hand and placed the other on her baby bump.

She was seven months pregnant.

Raul rented out the back room of a restaurant called El Azteca for the celebration. A long table served food buffet style. Kara's famished family swarmed the line when the dishes were unveiled.

Kara stayed seated, needing a brief break from the lovely parade of hugs. Her family members liked to hug with aggression. Their affection was sometimes so intense it hurt, though she wouldn't have traded it for anything. She looked around at all of those who had come up to California to watch her become a citizen and she felt an incomparable surge of love. She was part of something. She was an important rung in an ever extending ladder of people and she adored her place in the process.

Kara looked down at her ever growing belly and felt ready to continue the natural passing of the torch from one generation to the next.

She looked up at Carmen and her family. Her wonderful sister. She had always loved her but these past few years they had grown to be *friends* in a way she had never expected.

She looked up at her parents – paragons of humanity as far as she was concerned. She was so happy to be able to help them financially. They had done so much for her. She had finally told Juan about the extra money she was providing and Juan had reluctantly agreed to stop working. She could tell his pride was wounded but he was still immensely grateful to her. He hugged her and said, "I have raised a terrific girl."

She looked up at the man she would shortly marry, who already felt like her husband. Raul was indeed imperfect, as he had promised. But Kara loved him all the more for his imperfections. He was gentle and kind and sometimes oblivious and prone to unexpected short bursts of anger, but he was there for her every single moment of every single day. He loved her so thoroughly it was touching.

Raul was helping his children from his first marriage pass through the horde of starving Gomezs to get some food. He pushed them past Carlos, Ian, and Luis, the much more aggressive kids from Tijuana. She felt she loved Raul's kids just as much as she would love her own. Lizzie and she had hit it off from the start and Nick even seemed to grow fond of her over time. Nick actually reminded Kara of Dan, though she did not mention that to Raul.

She looked over at Dan. She looked at Dan and she felt…

"I am very happy for you Kara," said a voice to her right.

Her thought process was put on pause.

She turned her head. Ramon had wheeled himself next to her.

"Thanks Ramon," she said.

"I got you a gift."

"You didn't have to do that."

He lifted a bag into his lap. He pulled out a fancy looking bottle of tequila.

"This is rare and very fine stuff," he said. "I want you and Raul to enjoy over the years. Don't let him drink all of it if he gets upset after one argument."

Kara laughed, hoping, as was common, that Ramon's statement was a joke.

"Thank you, that is very generous," she said, accepting the gift.

"And I know that you're not much of a drinker, so in case Raul does most of the enjoying, I got you something else."

Raul handed her a long black jewelry box. Inside was a beautiful necklace.

"Ramon! This is not necessary!"

"It is necessary. You are my family now. You've got my great nephew in there," he said, indicating her bump.

"Or niece," she said.

"Yes, or niece."

"Thank you Ramon," she said emphatically.

"You are welcome. You're a real pro Kara. You deserve everything that comes to you."

Kara felt unexpectedly teary. She leaned in and gave Ramon a big hug.

When she separated from him, he wiped his hand across his forehead, clearing away mock sweat.

"Whew!" he said. "Remind me to give you jewelry more often."

She rolled her eyes – that old affectionate gesture.

"Now if you don't mind," he said, "I think I need a drink myself."

He wheeled himself out of the back room, seeking out the bar.

Dan stood by himself at the side of the room, drinking a glass of rum. He looked at Kara. He supposed he should really approach her. They had only thus far exchanged a brief hello from a distance.

He looked at her and he thought of how things could have happened differently. It could have been his child growing inside of her if he had wanted it.

It wasn't what he wanted. Not then and not now. That didn't stop him from wondering what it might have been like.

It also didn't stop him from missing her.

Dan was interrupted from his musings by the approach of Kara's father. For a second, he felt a brief flutter of fear, like a teenage boy caught in the bed of a girl by her imposing father.

"Daniel," said Juan. "I wanted to thank you."

Dan nodded. He let the tension evaporate, trying to hide the fact he ever felt it. Nevertheless, he was unsure where this interaction was going.

"You took care of my little girl," said Juan. "You did a good thing for her."

*Oh.* Dan felt naïve for imagining his marriage with Kara might still be taken seriously in the Gomez household. Of course they would know the truth by now. He was gratified to hear that Juan did not hate him for it.

"I'm sorry," said Dan. He felt the need to apologize, despite Juan's apparent warmth.

Juan held up his hand to indicate that such remorse was unnecessary. The man had a power to him. His simple gesture made Dan feel like a child forgiven for a misdeed by his loving parent. His own mother and father departed, it was not a feeling he had experienced for a long time.

"You did what she needed you to do. You will always be family."

"Thank you Mr. Gomez."

They shook hands.

Juan walked off. Dan looked back towards Kara. She was looking back at him, likely wondering about his interaction with her father.

No more putting it off. He was about to walk over to her when she got up from her seat and beat him to it.

Kara hugged him. He hugged her back. They held on for perhaps a little too long. Neither of them really wanted to separate, but they eventually did as they knew they must.

"Congratulations Lovey. And not just for the ceremony today."

He motioned to her belly.

"Yes," she said. "Thank you."

"How long?"

"Two more months."

"You're going to be a great mom."

She smiled.

"Thanks for coming all the way from New York," she said.

"Of course. Anything for my wife."

They both let that word hang in the air for a moment as memories of what was gone passed in between them.

"Are you seeing anyone?" Kara asked.

"Well…yeah, actually I am."

Dan had been dating a woman named Amy for several months. Almost as long as he had been with Kara actually, though it didn't feel close to it. He liked Amy a lot. It was different though. Their coupling didn't have the same *necessity* as his and Kara's had. Yet he was happy with her and he figured that was what mattered.

"That's good," said Kara, sounding both happy and sad about the news. She was surprised by her own mixed reaction and tried to tuck away any unwarranted jealousy. After all, she was about to legally divorce Dan. And she genuinely did want him to be happy with someone else.

"She's a very sweet girl, but she could never replace you," Dan said. "No one could."

Kara blushed. "Thank you my love."

"Raul got you quite the gorgeous engagement ring," he said, pointing to the gleaming diamond on her finger.

"Yes, it is nice."

"You're a citizen now. We'll get that quickie divorce and that will be that."

"How long are you staying?"

"Not long. I'm going down to San Diego tomorrow to see my sister."

"Your sister? The one you had not talked to in so long?"

"Yeah, I got back in touch with her. You were right of course. It was uncomfortable at first but it was worth it. Family is important."

"I am happy for you Daniel. That is wonderful."

Their conversation was put on halt by a fork loudly clinking against a glass.

Raul stood at the head of the room, ready to deliver a toast.

"I want to thank everyone for coming here today," he said. "Of course we're all here, because we all love Kara. We all know just how selfless and generous she is. She's always there for all of us, so today let's honor her and her great accomplishments. Please raise your glasses with me!"

The room did as asked. Dan raised his glass of rum.

"To Kara!" he said.

"TO KARA!" the room repeated.

"And now," said Raul. "Let's dance!"

He hit play on a speaker system and salsa music began to play. The party's members cheered, dropped their food, and got right to dancing with full, unrestrained, vigor.

Kara laughed with glee. Overwhelming love surged through her once again. It was moments like this, thought Kara, when it felt so incredibly clear why all of life's hardest moments were worth struggling through.

There was so much *good*. Yes, she was happy to learn, sometimes things in life *do* work out.

Even if certain sacrifices have to be made…

She turned to look at Dan. She expected to resume their conversation. But he had other plans.

He was dancing. Fantastically.

"How did you learn that!?" she asked, in shock.

"I took lessons," said Dan.

"You took lessons?"

Then Kara understood. He didn't need to say it. He had taken lessons for her. He had learned for her.

"Care to dance?" he said.

He held out his hand.

She looked over at Raul. He was dancing enthusiastically with Lizzie. He looked over towards Kara and shook his head with a smirk, indicating that he would join her as soon as his daughter would let him.

She turned back to Dan. She took his hand.

**ABOUT THE AUTHOR:**

*Jeremy Dorfman is a graduate of New York University's Tisch School of the Arts.*
*He can be contacted at jid204@gmail.com*